QUICK SERVICE

P. G. Wodehouse

QUICK
SERVICE

Barrie & Jenkins, London

Barrie & Jenkins Ltd
3 Fitzroy Square, London W1P 6JD

An imprint of the Hutchinson Publishing Group

London Melbourne Sydney Auckland
Wellington Johannesburg and agencies
throughout the world

First published by Herbert Jenkins Ltd 1940
This impression 1980

ISBN 0 257 66178 6

Printed and bound in Great Britain by
REDWOOD BURN LIMITED
Trowbridge & Esher

IN spite of the invigorating scent of coffee which greeted him as he opened the door, it was with drawn face and dull eye that the willowy young man with the butter-coloured hair and rather prominent Adam's apple entered the breakfast-room of Claines Hall, the Tudor mansion in Sussex recently purchased by Mrs. Howard Steptoe of Los Angeles. He yielded to no one in his appreciation of coffee, and a couple of cups would unquestionably go down all right, but nothing could alter the fact that on the previous evening he had got engaged to be married to a girl without a bean and was going to London this morning to break the news to his trustee. Even in the most favourable circumstances he did not enjoy meeting his trustee: and when compelled to vex and agitate that human snapping turtle, as he feared would be the case today, he always found himself regretting that his late father had not placed his financial affairs in the hands of some reasonably genial soul like Jack the Ripper.

The breakfast-room was bright and cheerful. Its French windows caught the morning sun. One of its walls displayed an old Flemish tapestry of boors revelling, another an old Flemish tapestry of boors taking it easy for a bit. Silver dishes warmed by little flames smiled from the sideboard, and beside them, as yet untouched by knife, the eye detected a large new ham. Over the fireplace there hung a striking portrait of a majestic woman in the early forties, who stared haughtily from the frame as if surprised and displeased by something she had seen in the middle distance. It was the work of a young artist named Jocelyn Weatherby, and its subject was Mrs. Chavender, widow of Mrs. Steptoe's brother Otis.

Mrs. Steptoe herself, a wiry little person with hard blue eyes, sat at the head of the table, instructing Sally Fairmile in her duties for the day. Sally was a poor relation, and as such always had plenty to occupy her time. When Mrs. Steptoe gave the orphan daughters of distant cousins a home, she liked them to earn their board and keep.

7

"Good morning, Lord Holbeton," she said absently.

"Good morning," said Sally, giving him a quick smile. This was the first she had seen of him since last night, when they had become engaged.

"Oh, good morning, good morning," said Lord Holbeton. "Good morning," he added, driving the thing home, and made for the sideboard in the hope of finding something there that would fortify the spirit.

"I'm sort of wondering," Mrs. Steptoe went on, as her guest seated himself after dishing out a moody portion of scrambled eggs, "how to fit everybody in today. About the cars, I mean. You're going to London, you told me?"

Lord Holbeton winced.

"Yes," he said, with a quiver in his voice. "Got to see a man about something."

"And Beatrice has to go to Brighton to present those prizes. She will want the Rolls. And the Packard is having something done to it. You'll have to have the two-seater. It's kind of rattly, but it moves. Sally can drive you. She's going in to get another valet for Howard."

Although he was aware that his hostess possessed the stuff in large quantities and denied her husband nothing, this surprised Lord Holbeton. It seemed to him to strike a note of almost wanton luxury, the sort of thing that causes French Revolutions and Declines and Falls of Roman Empires.

"How many does he have?" he asked, startled.

"Only one at a time," said Sally. "But he sort of runs through them."

"They don't like his manner," explained Mrs. Steptoe.

Lord Holbeton could sympathize with the honest fellows. He did not like Mr. Steptoe's manner himself. There had been something in the nature of an informal understanding, when he had come to stay at Claines Hall, that he should take his host in hand and give him a much-needed spot of polish. But so unpleasant had been the spirit in which the other had received his ministrations that he had soon abandoned this missionary work. Mr. Steptoe, when you tried to set his feet on the path that led to elegance and refinement, had a way of narrowing his eyes and saying "Ah, nerts!" out of the corner of his mouth, which would have discouraged Emily Post.

"When that last fellow quit," said Mrs. Steptoe, stirring her coffee grimly and looking a little like a rattlesnake, if one can imagine a rattlesnake stirring coffee, "he thought he had finally fought off the challenge. But he's living in a fool's paradise. As long as there's a valet left in England, Howard gets him. I've been telling Sally to hire a real tough specimen this time, the sort that'll stand no nonsense. I intend to smarten him up, if it's the last thing I do."

Mr. Steptoe came in as she spoke, an enormous mass of a man with a squashed nose and ears like the handles of an old Greek vase. He has been in once before, as a matter of fact, but Mrs. Steptoe had sent him out again to go and put a collar on. His air, which was sullen, made it plain that both in neck and spirit he was chafing under this treatment. Directing a lowering glance of dislike at Lord Holbeton, whom he considered a palooka of the first water and suspected of putting these ideas into his wife's head, he went to the sideboard and helped himself largely to fish.

The only member of the party still absent was Mrs. Chavender, the lady of the portrait. She entered a moment later, looking like Mrs. Siddons in one of her more regal rôles. She would have made a good subject for the brush of Sir Peter Lely or Sir Joshua Reynolds. Indeed, both Sir Joshua and Sir Peter would probably have made even a better job of her than Joss Weatherby had done—as Joss would have been the first to admit, for he was quite free from artistic jealousy.

Sweeping into the room with an air, she got a big reception.

"Good morning, Beatrice," said Mrs. Steptoe, beaming.

"Good morning, Mrs. Chavender," said Sally.

"Oh, hullo, hullo," said Lord Holbeton.

Mr. Steptoe said nothing. He had cocked an eye at the newcomer. That was as far as he was prepared to go. A simple child of nature, he believed, when at meals, in digging in and getting his. He reached out a hairy hand for the butter, and started lathering another slice of toast.

Lord Holbeton had sprung to his feet, a thing Mr. Steptoe would not have done in a million years, and was heading gallantly for the sideboard. It was those perfect manners of his, combined with his delicate good looks and the way he had of sitting down at the piano after dinner and singing such songs as *Trees* in a soft, quivery tenor voice, that had first attracted Sally Fairmile.

"What can I get you, Mrs. Chavender? Eggs? Fish? Ham?"

It was a moment big with fate. On this woman's answer hung

the destinies not only of all those present, but in addition of J. B. Duff, managing director of the firm of Duff and Trotter, London's leading provision merchants; of Joss Weatherby, the artist; of Chibnall, Mrs. Steptoe's butler; and of Vera Pym, barmaid at the Rose and Crown in the neighbouring town of Loose Chippings, Chibnall's *fiancée*.

If she had said "Eggs," nothing would have happened. Had she replied "Fish," the foundations of this little world would have remained unrocked.

"Ham," said Mrs. Chavender.

Lord Holbeton carved the ham with the polished elegance which marked all his actions, and silence fell upon the room, broken only by a crackling sound like a forest fire, as Mr. Steptoe champed his toast. This gorilla-jawed man could get a certain amount of noise-response even out of mashed potatoes, but it was when eating toast that you caught him at his best.

The conversational ball was eventually set rolling again by Mrs. Chavender. She had lowered her knife and fork, and was staring at her plate with a sort of queenly disgust, like Mrs. Siddons inspecting a caterpillar in her salad.

"This ham," she said, "is uneatable."

Mrs. Steptoe looked up in quick concern. Wealthy though she was herself, the moods of this still more opulent sister-in-law were of urgent importance to her. Like Ben Bolt's Alice, she trembled with fear at her frown. Mrs Chavender was understood to have a weak heart, and Mrs. Steptoe was her only relative.

"Is there something wrong with it, Beatrice?"

"Considering that I have just described it as uneatable, you may take it that it is not wholly without blemish."

"You bought it, Sally," said Mrs. Steptoe accusingly.

Sally was unable to deny the charge.

"I thought it was bound to be all right", she pleaded in defence. "It came from the best people in London."

"The question of their morals," said Mrs. Chavender, "does not arise. They may, as you say, be the best people in London, though that isn't saying much. My point is that they sell inferior ham. And let me tell you that I know ham. Before I married my late husband, I was engaged to a Ham King—though at that stage in his career I suppose one would have described him as a Ham Prince—and he talked of nothing else from morning till night. So I have had a thorough grounding. I shall go and see these crooks and lodge a strong complaint. Who are the swindling hounds?"

"Duff and Trotter," said Sally. "They are supposed to be the absolute final word in breakfast foodings. I must say I'm surprised that they should have taken advantage of a young girl's inexperience."

At the mention of that name, a sharp exclamation had escaped Lord Holbeton. He was sitting staring, apparently aghast, the scrambled eggs frozen upon his lips.

"Duff and Trotter?" he quavered.

"Duff and Trotter?" echoed Mrs. Chavender. It seemed to Sally that there was elation and triumph in her handsome eyes. She was looking like a Roman Matron who has unexpectedly backed the winning chariot at the Circus Maximus. "Are you telling me, my child, that this loathsome substance is one of Jimmy Duff's Paramount Hams?"

"Yes, that's what they're called."

Mrs. Chavender drew a deep breath.

"It's too good to be true," she said. "I didn't know that righteous retribution like this ever happened outside moral stories for children. Jimmy Duff is the man I was speaking of, Mabel—the one who sold hams and talked of nothing else. Words cannot describe the agonies of boredom he used to inflict on me. Jimmy Duff! James by golly Buchanan Duff! Well, well, well! I haven't seen Jimmy in fifteen years, and by the time I'm through with him he'll hope that our next get-together won't be for another thirty."

"What do you mean?"

"I propose to call on him this morning and let him know what a decent-minded woman thinks of his ghastly hams."

"But you are going to Brighton."

"I can take Jimmy en route."

"Wouldn't it be better to write?"

"Write? You don't seem to understand the position. Fifteen years ago, when I met Jimmy Duff and fell for his smooth city ways, I was a young, idealistic girl, all sentiment and romance. This sentiment and romance he blunted for ever with these foul hams of his. He used to take me out in the moonlight and tell me what gave them that nutty flavour. He would wait till the band was playing "Träumerei" and then describe the process of curing. And now, when after all these weary years I've a chance to get my own back, you tell me to write. Write indeed! I'm going to call at his office and look him in the eye and slap this ham down on his desk and watch him curl up at the edges. Ring for Chibnall."

The butler entered. A lissom, athletic young butler of the modern type. Dignified but sinewy.

"Chibnall, will you pack half a dozen slices of this ham in a cardboard box and put them in the car. And I'd better have the car a little earlier, if I'm to go to Brighton via London."

"Tell Purkis, Sally," said Mrs. Steptoe resignedly.

Sally rose obligingly. It was not till she was halfway to the garage that a bleating noise behind her told her that she had been followed by her betrothed.

"I say, Sally!"

"Oh, hullo, George," she said, turning quickly, like a startled kitten. She was conscious of a certain embarrassment. They had not been alone together since the emotional scene on the previous night, and she was thinking that it might not be easy to strike exactly the right note.

She need have had no concern. Lord Holbeton was far too agitated to be critical about right notes. His eye was wild, his mouth hung ajar, and his Adam's apple was gambolling like a lamb in springtime.

"I say, Sally, this is absolutely frightful!"

"What?"

"This Chavender woman and the ham business."

"I thought it rather funny."

"Funny? Ha!" said Lord Holbeton, doing a bitter dance-step. "You won't think it so bally funny when you hear the facts in the case." He paused for an instant to overcome his feelings. The position of affairs which he was about to outline was one that had frequently caused the iron to enter into his soul. "I didn't tell you last night, but my guv'nor, when he died, left me a pot of money."

Sally was perplexed. She was not a mercenary girl, but she had served quite a long sentence as a Steptoe poor relation, and she could see nothing in this fact to depress the spirits.

"Well, surely that's fine? I love the stuff."

"Yes, but there's a catch. He left it in trust. Having got it into his head that I wasn't fit to have a pot of money——"

"What made him think that?"

Actually, what had given the first Baron this poor opinion of a once-adored son had been that unfortunate breach of promise case at Oxford, but Lord Holbeton felt that it might be injudicious to mention this.

"Oh, I don't know. Guv'nors get these ideas. Anyway, he left the stuff in trust. I can't finger a fiver except by showing good and substantial cause to my trustee. And do you know who he is—this blighted trustee? Old Duff. The fellow this woman's going to slap down slices of ham in front of."

"But how does he come to be mixed up with you?"

"My guv'nor was his partner. His name was Trotter before he got his title. He always thought a lot of old Duff, so he made him my trustee. And I was planning to tackle him this morning and tell him about us and try to get some cash out of him. And now this happens."

"I see what you mean," said Sally thoughtfully. "You think he won't be in melting mood after Mrs. Chavender's visit?"

"Well, is it likely?"

"I suppose it isn't."

"If," said Lord Holbeton, "the old blister has consistently refused to cough up hitherto, will he unbelt at a moment when his soul is all gashed by this frightful female's taunts and sneers? He loves those hams of his like sons. What are those things sheep have?"

"Lambs?"

"Yes, but some special breed of lambs."

"Ewe lambs?"

"That's right. The Paramount Ham is old Duff's ewe lamb. He started out with it, and the rest of the business means nothing to him. A nice frame of mind he'll be in to listen to the voice of reason after seeing Mrs. Chavender."

It is the woman's part at times like this to stimulate and encourage.

"Oh, you'll be able to talk him round," said Sally hopefully.

"You think so?"

"Yes."

"I don't," said Lord Holbeton. "And I'll tell you why. Because I'm not going within fifty ruddy miles of him."

"Oh, George!"

"And, added Lord Holbeton, "it's no good saying 'Oh, George.' I'd rather hobnob with a wounded puma."

"But he isn't as terrible as all that."

"You've never seen him."

"I've seen his picture. When you buy a Paramount Ham, you get it thrown in, on the wrapper. I thought he looked an old pet."

Lord Holbeton blinked.

"An old pet?"

"Yes."

"An old *pet*?" said Lord Holbeton, still not quite sure that he had heard aright. "What about those eyebrows?"

"Rather dressy. I admired them."

Lord Holbeton decided to abandon a fruitless discussion. On the subject of J. Buchanan Duff, it was plain that this girl and he were poles apart and could never hope to find a formula.

"Well, if that's how you feel," he said, "why don't *you* go and tackle him?"

"All right," said Sally. "I will."

Lord Holbeton stared. His question had been intended in a purely satirical spirit, and her literal acceptance of it stunned him. For an instant, compunction gripped him. She seemed so young, so frail to go up against one who even on his good mornings resembled something out of the Book of Revelations.

Then there swept over him the thought of what a lot of unpleasantness this would save him. If somebody had to go over Niagara Falls in a barrel, how much more agreeable if it were not he.

"You don't mean that?"

"I do."

"Will you really?"

"Certainly. Who's afraid?"

"Be prepared for those eyebrows."

"I'm looking forward to them."

"You might be able to get to him before Mrs. Chavender."

"Not if she's in the Rolls and I'm in the two-seater."

"No, that's true. Then we must just hope for the best."

"That's what we must hope for."

"And all this," said Lord Holbeton, "could have been avoided, if only the woman had taken scrambled eggs. That's Life, I suppose."

"That's Life," agreed Sally.

THE premises of Duff and Trotter, those human benefactors at the mention of whose name every discriminating Londoner raises a reverent hat, occupy an island site in the neighbourhood of Regent Street. The patron enters through a swing door, and having done so finds himself in a sort of cathedral given over to a display of the merchandise which has made the firm famous. Here are pies; there fruit; over yonder soups and groceries; further on, jams, marmalades, caviares and potted meats. The Paramount Ham, in its capacity of ewe lamb to the managing director, has a shrine to itself.

Most of the Duff and Trotter business being conducted over the telephone, one finds here none of the squash and bustle of baser establishments. Only a sprinkling of Duchesses with watering mouths and a few Earls licking their lips were present at eleven o'clock that morning when Joss Weatherby came in and started to thread his way through the groves of eatables.

Joss Weatherby did the posters for Paramount Ham, a lean, cheerful, loose-limbed young man who bore up extraordinarily well under a task which might easily have soured one of a less ebullient temperament. This was probably due to the fact that he ate well, slept well and enjoyed a perfect digestion—in which respect he differed from his employer, whose alimentary canal gave him a good deal of trouble.

His course, as he headed for Mr Duff's private office on the second floor, took him past the fruits and vegetables, and though hampered by a large portfolio under one arm he was able with his free hand to collect a bunch of grapes and a custard apple while flitting by. The disposal of the last of the grapes synchronized with his arrival at the outer cubby-hole occupied by Miss Daphne Hesseltyne, Mr. Duff's secretary.

"Good morning, young Lollipop," he said courteously.

"Good evening," said Miss Hesseltyne, who had a great gift for repartee. "This is a nice time for coming in. You were supposed to be here at ten."

"I unfortunately overslept myself this morning. A man took me to one of those charity gambling places last night. You will be glad to hear that I cleaned up big in a crap game. Have a custard apple? It's on the house. The fruit and veg. department has just given of its plenty."

"Have you been pinching fruit again? You remember how Mr. Duff told you off last time."

"But this time I defied detection. My fingers just flickered."

"Well, you'd better go in. He's waiting for you. And let me tell you he's as cross as two sticks. He's got indigestion again."

"Poor, unhappy wreck. I sometimes feel the best thing he could do would be to throw himself away and start afresh. But he won't be cross with me. Not with lovable old Weatherby. Did I ever tell you that I once saved him from drowning back in America? Stick your head through the transom and watch how his face lights up when I appear."

The inner office was, however, empty when Joss entered. It was only after he had banged cheerily on the desk with a paper-weight, at the same time shouting a jovial "Bring out your dead," that Mr. Duff came in from the little balcony outside the window, where he had been attempting to alleviate his dyspepsia by deep breathing.

"Aha, J.B.," said Joss sunnily. "Good morrow."

"Oh, you're there, are you?" said Mr. Duff, making no attempt to emulate his junior's effervescence.

The managing director of Duff and Trotter was a large man who, after an athletic youth, had allowed himself to put on weight. In his college days, he had been a hammer-thrower of some repute, and he was looking as if he wished he had a hammer now and could throw it at Joss. The eyebrows of which Lord Holbeton had spoken so feelingly were drawn together in a solid line, and the eyes beneath them glared malignantly. They seemed to light up the room, and only a young man with the nerve of an Army mule, which Joss was fortunate enough to possess, could have met them without quailing.

"You're late! he boomed.

"Not really," said Joss.

"What the devil do you mean, not really?"

"A man like me always seems to be later than he is. That is because people sit yearning for him. They get all tense, listening for his footstep, and every minute seems an hour. Well, J.B., they tell me you've got the collywobbles again. If true, too bad."

"You were supposed to be here at ten."

"As I was just explaining to the Hesseltyne half-portion, I overslept myself. I got into a crap game last night, and swept through the opposition like a devouring flame. You would have been proud of me."

"So you gamble, do you?"

"Only once in a blue moon. I wish you wouldn't talk as if I were a Greek Syndicate. Well, now to business. I've brought you my sketches for the new posters of ye Ham Paramount. I don't know if they're any good."

"They aren't."

"You've not seen them."

"I don't have to."

Joss eyed him coldly. He was extremely fond of his employer, but he inclined to the view that it would do him all the good in the world if somebody occasionally kicked him in the stomach.

"I don't know if you know it, J.B., but you're the sort of fellow who causes hundreds to fall under suspicion when he's found stabbed in his library with a paper-knife of Oriental design."

Mr. Duff stiffened.

"I don't know if *you* know it, young man, but you get fresher and fresher every time I see you. And you were fresh enough to start with. If this sort of thing goes on, I shall fire you."

"Nonsense. Why, I saved your life."

"Yes, and the way I'm feeling this morning, I'd like to sue you. Well?"

The question was addressed to Miss Hesseltyne, who had entered from her outer lair.

"There's a lady to see you, Mr. Duff."

"Heavily veiled and diffusing a strange, exotic scent," said Joss. "I suppose they're in and out of here all the time."

"Could you shut your trap for a moment?" asked Mr. Duff.

"I suppose so, if it's absolutely necessary," said Joss.

"Who is she?"

"Her name is Mrs. Chavender."

"What!"

It was as if Miss Hesseltyne had struck her overlord with a meat axe. He rocked back on his heels and seemed to give at every joint.

Joss was frowning thoughtfully.

"Chavender? Chavender? I know a Mrs. Chavender. I wonder if it's the same. Tell her to come right up."

Mr. Duff barked like a sea-lion.

"Don't you do anything of the sort. What do you mean, giving orders in my office? Say I'm out."

"Yes, sir."

Joss was surprised.

"Why this coyness, J.B.? If it's the Mrs. Chavender I know, you'll like her. She's a terrific old sport. I painted her portrait at Palm Beach two years ago."

Miss Hesseltyne re-entered.

"I couldn't get the lady, sir, to tell her. She was on her way up."

Mr. Duff had begun to exhibit all the mannerisms of a trapped creature of the wild.

"I'm off!"

"You'll meet her in the passage," said Joss, and Mr. Duff paused with his fingers on the door handle. Joss, though still at a loss, felt a pang of compassion.

"Well, I can't follow your thought processes, J.B., but if you really wish to elude this very charming lady, you'd better hop out on to the balcony. I'll close the window behind you."

The advice seemed admirable to Mr. Duff. He shot out like a rabbit. He had scarcely disappeared, when there was a brisk bang upon the door and the visitor sailed into the room. In her right hand, like the banner with the strange device, she bore a cardboard box.

Expecting to see Mr. Duff and finding in his stead a beardless stripling, Mrs. Chavender seemed taken aback.

"Hullo, where's Jimmy?"

"He has had to step out for a moment."

"And who are you?"

"His best friend and severest critic. My name is Weatherby. I'm afraid you have forgotten me, Mrs. Chavender."

Mrs. Chavender had produced a lorgnette.

"Well, I'll be darned. You're the boy who painted my portrait."

"That's right. Have you still got it?"

"I gave it to my sister-in-law's husband, Howard Steptoe. I live with them. It's hanging in the breakfast-room."

"I'll bet it gives the household a rare appetite. One look at it, and they're in among the eggs and bacon like wolves."

"I see you're still as fresh as ever."

"It's odd how people persist in describing me as fresh. I should have said that I just had a sort of easy affability of manner. Mr. Duff was complaining of my freshness only this morning. It seemed to be spoiling his day."

"Do you work for him?"

"He would tell you I didn't, but I do, like a beaver. I'm one of the staff artists."

"From what you say, it sounds as if he had become a grouch. Is he married?"

"No."

"Then that's the trouble. That's what made him curdle. Every man ought to be married."

"You never spoke a truer word."

"Are you?"

"Not yet. I'm still waiting for the right girl. When she comes along, you will see quick service."

Mrs. Chavender regarded him critically.

"You're not a bad-looking young hound."

"Surely a conservative way of putting it?"

"What's Jimmy like these days? He had his moments, when I knew him."

"Traces of the old fascination remain. In a dim light he still casts a spell. I'll draw you a picture of him, shall I?"

The sketch which Joss dashed off on a piece of Duff and Trotter notepaper was a hasty one and leaned somewhat in the direction of caricature, but Mrs. Chavender greeted it with appreciative cries.

"That's Jimmy, all right. But you've made him happier looking than he will be when I see him."

"I beg your pardon?"

"He'll be dancing with tears in his eyes, believe me. Cast a glance at this."

Joss peered into the cardboard box.

"It looks like ham."

"Yes, let's be fair. I suppose there is a sort of superficial resemblance. It's a clipping from one of Jimmy's Paramounts. I've come to complain about it."

Joss looked swiftly at the ceiling. It had not fallen, but he felt that it must have been a near thing.

"Complain? About Paramount Ham?"

"It's a disgrace to a proud industry and an imposition on a

trusting public. Nine-tenths of it is flabby fat. The remainder appears to be composed of pink elastic."

"You weren't intending to tell J.B. that? You'll break his heart."

"I want to."

"Thank Heaven he's out."

"How long is he going to be out?"

"It may be for years or it may be for ever."

"And I can't wait, darn it. I've got to get to Brighton. I'm presenting the prizes at a girls' school. You'll have to act as my agent. Call me up and tell me how he took it. Loose Chippings 803 is the number. Or, if you prefer to write, the address is Claines Hall, Loose Chippings, Sussex. Well, I must be getting along. Nice to have seen you again. Listen, what do I say to a bunch of schoolgirls?"

" 'Hullo, girls,' or something like that?"

"That would be fine, if my speech hadn't got to last three-quarters of an hour and inspire them to become good wives and mothers. Oh, well, I guess I'll think of something on the way down."

Joss, returning from escorting her to the elevator, found that Mr. Duff had emerged from hiding. He was sitting at the desk, mopping his brow.

"Phew!" he said. "That was a narrow escape. Get me a glass of sherry."

"Sherry?"

"There's some in that cupboard over there."

"So you keep sherry in your cupboard, do you?" said Joss, interested. "Secret drinker, eh? Tell me, J.B., why didn't you want to meet Mrs. Chavender?"

A glassy, hunted look came into Mr. Duff's eyes.

"We were engaged to be married once."

"Ah!" said Joss, understanding. He knew his employer to be as sturdy a bachelor as ever shivered at the sound of a wedding bell. Sturdy bachelors, he was aware, are often averse from reunions with their old loves.

"I don't like this business of her calling at my office," said Mr. Duff, restoring himself with sherry. "It's sinister. What did she want? I couldn't hear a thing out there."

Joss decided to be humane. No need to break his portly butterfly on the wheel by revealing the truth.

"She just wanted to see you and say hullo."

"We haven't met in fifteen years."

"Ah, but you're like the chewing-gum. The taste lingers."

"She looks just the same."

"You saw her?"

"Yes, I peeked in. Not changed a scrap. Same eyes. Same curling lips. Well, never mind that," said Mr. Duff, recalling himself to the present. His eye took on its office hours expression.

"Let's see those sketches."

Joss opened the portfolio, and tilted its contents on to the desk. There were half a dozen sketches, each showing a saucer-eyed girl, her face split by a wide grin. He arranged them in a row before his employer.

"You remind me of an Oriental monarch surrounded by his harem," he said genially. "The Sultan looks them over."

Mr. Duff was scanning the drawings with a captious eye.

"Awful," he said.

"Lovely line work," Joss pointed out. "Who is this man Weatherby? He's good."

Mr. Duff continued peevish.

"It's these damned girls. I'm sick of them."

"Now there," said Joss, sitting on the corner of the desk and rising immediately at his employer's request, "I am with you, J.B., heart and soul. The whole trouble is, I am hampered and shackled by the Mandarins of the Art Department. They won't allow me to fulfil myself. I don't know if you have ever seen a glorious eagle spreading its wings for a flight into the empyrean only to discover that it is tied by the leg to a post, but that's me. 'Girls!' say the Mandarins. 'Let us have girls with big eyes and lots of teeth, radiantly full of Paramount Ham,' and I have to do it. Personally, I have never been able to see why the fact that a goggle-eyed girl with buck teeth likes the stuff should carry the slightest weight with an intelligent public. But there it is."

There had been slowly dawning on Mr. Duff's face during this harangue a sort of Soul's Awakening look. It was not unfamiliar to Joss. Combined with the portentous waggling of his eyebrows and the general swelling of his person, it told him that the other had been seized by one of the bright thoughts that came to him from time to time. Mr. Duff, he perceived, was now the Napoleon of Commerce, the man with the lightning mind who gets things done.

"Hey!"

"Yes, J.B.?"

"I've had an idea."

"I thought I noticed something fermenting."

"These girls. The public is sick of them. They want something different."

"Just what I tell the Mandarins."

"New note."

"Exactly."

"Do you know what I'm going to do?"

"Sack the lot and make me head of the Art Department."

"You'll be doing well if you hold the job you've got."

"Oh, I don't think we need have any uneasiness about that."

"Don't you? Well, listen. Here's what I'm going to do. Came to me all in a flash. Instead of a fat-headed flapper saying 'Hurrah! It's Paramount Ham!' I'm going to give them Beatrice Chavender curling her lip and saying: 'Take this damned stuff away. I want *Paramount!*' "

Loath though he was to encourage his employer in any way lest he get above himself, Joss was forced to drop a word of approval.

"It's a thought," he agreed.

"Sninspiration," corrected Mr. Duff.

"Yes, I see what you mean. I've been thinking along those lines myself. Somebody like Mrs. Chavender——"

"I didn't say somebody like Mrs. Chavender, I said Mrs. Chavender. You say you painted a portrait of her. Was it good?"

"My dear J.B., need you ask?"

"It got that expression of hers?"

"Perfectly."

"Then it would make a great poster?"

"No question about that. It would send every thinking housewife in England rushing to her grocer like a stampeding mustang, screaming for the stuff."

"Well, that's what I'm saying. That portrait is our new poster."

Joss regarded him with frank astonishment. When Mr. Duff came over all executive and began to get bright ideas for gingering up the business, he was apt to be startling, but hitherto he had never touched quite these heights.

"You aren't serious?"

"Of course, I'm serious."

"You can't do it."

"Why can't I?"

"Well, for one thing, she would bring an action and mulct you in sensational damages."

"Let her. I'll charge it off to advertising expenses."

"And then, of course, there are the ordinary human decencies to be thought of."

Mr. Duff declined to consider these.

"Has she still got that portrait?"

"She tells me she gave it to the husband of her sister-in-law, with whom she lives—a Mrs. Steptoe of Claines Hall, Loose Chippings, Sussex."

"Have Miss Hesseltyne find out the number."

"I know it. Loose Chippings 803."

"Then I'll call up this Steptoe from the club, and see if we can do a deal. I'm going to my osteopath now. He may be able to do something for this indigestion of mine."

"That's the spirit. Up the Duffs! But, listen, J.B.——"

"If I'm wanted, his name's Clunk."

"You won't be wanted whatever his name is. You won't be missed for a minute. Nobody'll know you've gone."

"Fresher and fresher and fresher," sighed Mr. Duff.

"But listen, J.B.—about this portrait."

"I don't want any argument."

"I was merely going to say—"

"Well, don't. That's the trouble with you—always has been—you talk too much."

Joss shrugged his shoulders. To attempt to reason further would, he saw, be a waste of time. His companion had spoken of this project of his as an idea, but J. B. Duff did not get ideas, he got obsessions, and on these occasions was like the gentleman in the poem who on honeydew had fed and drunk the milk of Paradise. You just said: "Beware, beware! His flashing eyes, his floating hair!" and wove a circle round him thrice, and that was practically all you could do about it.

"Well, all right," he said. "Carry on, carry on. But don't forget I told you."

"Told me what?"

"I don't know. Something, probably."

Mr. Duff fell into a momentary reverie. He emerged from it

with a rumbling chuckle. A random thought seemed to have pleased him.

"Shall I tell *you* something?"

"Do."

"Here's where the joke comes in. Beatrice never liked those hams."

"No?"

"No. That's what we split up about. Gosh, how it all comes back to me. It was a summer night, and we were walking by the seashore. There was a moon, I remember, and everything was very still, except for a fellow in the distance singing some old love song to the guitar. And I was just telling her how the sales of the Paramount in New York State compared with those in Illinois, when she suddenly turned on me like a tigress and shouted: 'You and your darned old hams!' and swept off and married Otis Chavender, Import and Export. Thank God!" said Mr. Duff piously.

Joss, as we have seen, held decided views on romance. Though he had never yet met a girl on whom he could feel justified in pouring out the full ardour of a richly emotional nature, he was a modern troubadour. It was with a good deal of abhorrence that he stared at this earthy man.

"I don't want to hurt your feelings, J.B." he said, "but you have the soul of a wart-hog. And not a very nice wart-hog, either."

"You're fired."

"No, I'm not. Don't start clowning now. The trouble with you is that it's anything for a laugh. Do you mean you really like being a bachelor?"

"I love it."

"You must be crazy. Me," said Joss softly, "I dream all the time of some sweet girl who will some day come into my life like a tender goddess and gaze into my eyes and put a hand on each cheek and draw my face down to hers and whisper: 'My man!' "

'Brrh!" said Mr. Duff. "Don't talk of such things. You give me the creeps."

Left alone, Joss moved over to the chair whose soft cushions were pressed as a rule only by the sacred Duff trouser-seat. Having reclined there for some moments, thinking of this and that, he touched the bell sharply, and was pleasantly entertained when Miss Hesseltyne came bursting in, all zeal and notebook.

"Merely a practice alarm to test your efficiency, young Lollipop," he explained. "You may withdraw."

He nestled into the chair again, and placed his feet on the desk. It was becoming increasingly apparent to him that the head of the firm of Duff and Trotter had one of those jobs which may be grouped for purposes of convenience under the general heading of velvet. Nearly a quarter of an hour had passed since the big chief had left him, and absolutely nothing had come up in the way of delicate problems calling for instant decision. He had always had a suspicion that these tycoons earned their money easily.

It was as he was beginning to feel a little bored by inaction that Miss Hesseltyne appeared in the doorway, causing him to raise his eyebrows sternly.

"I didn't ring."

"I know you didn't."

"Then why are you here? Go back, and I'll press the bell, and then you come in again. We must have system."

Miss Hesseltyne seemed stirred and excited.

"I told you so!" she said.

"What did you tell me?"

"The store detective saw you pinch that fruit."

"A murrain on the luck!"

"And he's going to report you to Mr. Duff directly he gets back."

Joss's face darkened.

"This is monstrous. Am I to swoon at my work for want of an occasional custard apple? Any doctor will tell you that a man needs a little something round about the middle of the morning. What is technically known as his elevenses. Otherwise the machine breaks down. I shall talk very straight to J.B. about this, when I see him. Am I in a provision bin or a concentration camp?"

He would have spoken further, but at this moment the bell rang in the outer office.

"See who that is," he said curtly. He had not meant to be curt, but the spiritual influence of J.B. Duff's chair was strong upon him.

"It's a lady to see Mr. Duff," said Miss Hesseltyne, returning.

"What, another? All right, show her in," said Joss, leaning back and putting the tips of his fingers together. "I can give her five minutes."

"Miss Fairmile," announced Miss Hesseltyne.

"Good morning," said Sally.

Joss shot from his chair like a jumping bean, and came to earth, quivering.

"Good morning," he said, speaking with some difficulty. For he was in love, and the thing had come upon him as a complete surprise.

★ 3 ★

JOSS WEATHERBY, as has been shown, was a young man a good
deal given to dreaming of the girl who would one day come
into his life and make it a thing of moonshine and roses, and for
some little while past he had made a practice of keeping an eye
fixed on the horizon in case she should appear. But he had never
expected her to pop up out of a trap like this. He was conscious
of a tingling of the limbs and a strange inability to breathe.

Resilience, however, was one of the leading features of his
interesting character. He began to recover. The mists cleared
from before his eyes, and the sensation of having been hit on the
head by a blunt instrument passed. If not yet actually back in
mid-season form, he was at least more himself and able to
scrutinize Sally carefully and in detail.

Odd, he was feeling, that she should be so small and slight. He
had always pictured this girl of his as rather on the tall side. And
her eyes, he had fancied, would be hazel. Why, he could not have
said. Just an idea.

Sally's, like Mrs. Steptoe's, were blue. But whereas the blue
eyes of Mrs Steptoe were light and gave the impression of being
constructed of some sort of chinaware, those of Sally Fairmile
were dark, like the sky on a summer night. Mrs. Steptoe's eyes
were capable of dinting armour plate, and in the case of more
yielding substances such as the soul of Howard Steptoe could go
right through and come out on the other side. Sally's were soft
and appealing. At least, they appealed to Joss.

He was able to observe this more readily because at the moment
she seemed all eyes. Now that she was so nearly face to face with
Lord Holbeton's formidable trustee, Sally had been gripped by a
sharp attack of panic.

She fought down the ignoble weakness. After all, she reminded
herself, on the wrapper of that ham he had looked an old
pet.

"I wanted to see Mr. Duff," she said.

Joss drew a deep breath. He remembered now that she had

27

spoken before, as she came into the room, but he had been so dazed just then that he had scarcely heard her. The discovery that in addition to her other perfections she had a musical voice filled him with a profound relief. The way things are in this world, he was telling himself, anyone as lovely as this girl would be sure to talk like a rasping file. Joss Weatherby had lived a hard and testing life, in which most of the things which looked good at first sight had proved to have a string attached to them.

He closed his eyes.

"Say that again."

"What?"

" 'I wanted to see Mr. Duff.' "

"Why?"

"You have such an amazingly attractive speaking voice. It reminds me of springtime and daffodils and young birds chirping on dewy lawns."

"Oh?" It was beginning to be borne in upon Sally that she was in the presence of an eccentric. "Well, that's fine, isn't it?"

"It suits me," said Joss.

There was a pause. Joss's eyes were still closed. His air was that of a music lover savouring the strains of some beautiful melody. Sally, regarding him, came to the conclusion that he looked rather nice. Crazy, apparently, but quite nice.

"Well, can I?"

Joss opened his eyes.

"I beg your pardon?"

"See Mr. Duff."

"He's out at the moment. Could I help you?"

"No, thanks."

"I am his right-hand man. If you've come to buy a game pie, I think I have sufficient influence to swing it for you."

"I'm afraid a right-hand man won't do. You see, it's a personal matter."

"He has no secrets from me."

"He's going to have this one," said Sally, and smiled a sudden smile which sent Joss rocking back on his heels as if the old blunt instrument had been applied again.

"You shouldn't do that without warning," he said reproachfully. "You ought to blow a horn or something. Are you resolved to see J.B.?"

"Yes, really."

"He's a bit fretful this morning. Teething, I think. Well, in that case, you ought to fortify yourself. Would you like a glass of sherry?"

"Thank you," said Sally gratefully.

"Unless the mice have been at it," said Joss, "it should be in this cupboard."

He filled the glasses. A sip satisfied him that J. B. Duff, that old tippler, was sound on sherry. This was a nice, nutty brand.

"Skin off your nose," he said politely.

"Skin off yours," said Sally. "What a perfect host you are."

"One has one's humane instincts. I couldn't let you go up against old Battler Duff without a bracer."

"Is he really so terrible?"

"Did you ever read *Pilgrim's Progress*?"

"As a child."

"Remember Apollyon straddling across the way?"

"Yes."

"Duff. More sherry?"

"Thank you."

"Mud in you eye."

"The same in yours. You've saved my life. I've had an exhausting morning."

"Shopping?"

"Trying to engage a valet."

"Any luck?"

"No. I shall have to go back after lunch."

"It shouldn't be so difficult to get a valet, if you try the right place. You went to a valetorium, I presume?"

"Yes, but I had been told to get a specially ferocious one. You see, Mr. Steptoe isn't easy to get on with."

"Did you say Steptoe?"

"Yes. I live with a Mrs. Steptoe. She's a sort of cousin."

"Not Mrs. Steptoe of Claines Hall, Loose Chippings, Sussex—telephone number Loose Chippings 803?"

"Yes. How odd that you should know."

"I've just been having a pleasant reunion with Mrs. Chavender. She and I are old buddies. Well, this is the most extraordinary thing. For years I have jogged along without so much as hearing of Claines Hall, and to-day—suddenly—without the slightest warning—I hear of nothing else. This must mean something. One seems to detect the hand of Fate."

Sally was not interested in the hand of Fate. She was anxious to be reassured on an important point.

"Did Mrs. Chavender see Mr. Duff?"

"No."

"Good!"

"Why? Not that I'm inquisitive, of course."

"No, I noticed that. It's just that there were reasons why I didn't want them to meet."

"Which were?"

"How nice it is that you're not inquisitive."

"I never have been, from a child. More sherry?"

"I have some, thanks."

"Then hey hey!"

"Hey hey!"

"HEY!" cried Mr. Duff, joining in the chorus from the doorway. Clunk, osteopath, did his torso-twisting at an address not very distant from the Duff and Trotter head-quarters, and he had been able to get there and back in nice quick time.

The mood in which J. B. Duff surveyed the scene before him was not a frolicsome one. Clunk, the old reliable, had given him a certain amount of physical relief, but this had been offset by the fact that his soul was feeling as if it had been churned up by an egg-whisk. It was no kindly purveyor of hams and groceries who now stood brooding over the revels, but to all intents and purposes a fiend with a hatchet.

To the stormy darkness of spirit from which he was suffering what had contributed most was the recent uncompromising rejection of his offer for the Chavender portrait. Establishing communication with Loose Chippings 803, he had been informed by a cold, metallic voice that Mrs. Steptoe was speaking, and a few moments later this voice, now colder and even more metallic had said "Certainly not!" adding that it had never heard of such a thing. The receiver at the Loose Chippings end had then been replaced with a good deal of wristy follow-through.

On top of this had come the store detective's conscientious report concerning Joss and the fruit. And now, hastening to the office to work off his pent-up venom on his erring employee, the first thing he saw as he opened the door was that young man presiding at what had all the appearance of an orgy. And simultaneously it dawned upon him that the basis of the orgy—what was making the part go—was his own personal sherry. Little

wonder that he emitted that tempestuous "Hey!" Many men in
his place would have said something stronger.

The ejaculation, shattering the momentary silence, affected the
two occupants of the room disagreeably. Sally, whose back was to
the door and who had been unaware of this addition to the
festivities, leaped as if a bomb had been touched off beneath her,
while Joss, rising more slowly, stood contemplating his employer
with an alert eye.

It was clear to him that a situation had arisen which called for
the promptest action. Miss Hesseltyne's communication had left
him in no doubt as to the nature of the harangue which would
follow that preliminary "Hey!". Once before, as she had reminded
him, Mr. Duff had spoken with a breezy frankness on the subject
of wage slaves who helped themselves to the store's fruit. And it
was the recollection of what he had said on that occasion that
decided Joss to act swiftly.

To approach Mr. Duff, and seize Mr. Duff by the shoulders
and give Mr. Duff what is familiarly known as the bum's rush was
with him the work of a moment.

"How dare you come in here and shout at me like that?" he
demanded sternly. "Upon my soul, the discipline in this place
gets worse every day. Excuse me," he said. "One of my staff.
Wants to see me about something. Back in a minute."

He strode from the room, propelling Mr. Duff before him, and
closed the door.

★ 4 ★

THE conversation that took place in the passage outside was not an extended one. Mr. Duff was temporarily incapable of speech, and Joss wanted to get back to Sally.

"J.B.," said Joss, "would you care to be torn limb from limb?"

Mr. Duff had begun to feel alarmed. He had never heard of a staff artist assaulting his employer, but everything has to have a beginning and Joss, he knew, had an original mind and would not allow himself to be deterred by mere lack of precedent.

"Because I'll tell you how you can work it. By going into that room and saying what you were intending to say. That girl in there is the most wonderful girl in the world, and if you think that I shall just stand saying 'Yes, sir' and 'No, sir' while you tick me off in her presence, you are mistaken, J.B., grievously mistaken. If you so much as shove your nose inside that door till you're sent for, I'll break your spine in eight places. You'll think you're back at the osteopath's."

He turned away with a severe glance, and Mr. Duff found speech.

"Hey!"

"Yes, Duff?"

"You're fired!"

"All right."

"Really fired, I mean."

"All right, all right," said Joss impatiently. "I haven't time to talk shop now."

He went back into the office.

"I'm so sorry," he said. "The trouble is, these fellows have no initiative. The least trifle that goes wrong they loose their heads and come running to me. It's 'Ask Mr. Weatherby,' 'Put it up to Mr. Weatherby,' 'Mr Weatherby will know,' all the time. I suppose it's the penalty one pays for having a certain grip of things, but it can be very annoying. I had to be a little terse with poor old Wapshott."

"Wapshott?"

32

"That was Wapshott. P. P. Wapshott, head of the pressed beef and *pâté de foie gras* department."

"How odd!"

"Why odd?"

"He looked to me just like Mr. Duff."

"But I gathered you had not met Mr. Duff."

"His picture is on the wrapper on Paramount Ham."

"Ah? I had forgotten that. Yes, you are quite right. It was Mr. Duff."

"What happened?"

"He fired me. And, do you know, I had a premonition that he would. I suppose I'm psychic."

Sally had been principally concerned with the probable effect of the recent activities on her own fortunes, reasoning correctly that a J.B. Duff who had just been bundled out of his office by the shoulder-blades would be in no mood to listen with sympathy to a tale of young love. She now forgot self. This pleasant, if half-witted, young man was in trouble, and she grieved for him.

"Oh, I am sorry."

"The loss is his."

"Why did you do it?"

"I had no option. A little unpleasantness has arisen this morning in connection with my habit of helping myself to samples from the fruit and veg. department, and I saw that he was about to deliver a set speech on the subject, coupled with the name of sherry. I naturally couldn't have him doing that in front of you. He's an outspoken old bird, and it would have been impossible for you, listening to him, to have retained the high opinion you have formed of me. At the moment when he entered the room, you were just saying to yourself 'What a splendid fellow this Mr. Weatherby is, to be sure! I can't remember ever meeting a man I admired more.' Two minutes of J. B. Duff's coarse abuse, and my glamour would have wilted like a salted snail."

"But what will you do?"

"You mean in the way of securing other employment? That's all right. I'm going to be Mr. Steptoe's valet."

"What!"

"You said the place was open."

"But you can't be a valet."

"Why not?"

"How can you?"

"By presenting myself at Claines Hall this afternoon in that capacity. You aren't going to tell me that you refuse to give me the nomination? If it hadn't been for you, I wouldn't be out of a job. There are such things as moral obligations. Do have some more sherry, won't you? This may be our last chance of enjoying J. B. Duff's hospitality."

Sally shook her head. She was thinking. If she was to secure something special in the way of gentlemen's personal gentlemen, as Mrs. Steptoe had enjoined upon her, this did seem an admirable opportunity of doing it.

It seemed, indeed, the only opportunity. The registry office that morning had been able to produce none but the softer and more fragile type of valet. Wispy young men with spaniel eyes and deferential manners had been paraded before her in large numbers, all probably admirable at folding, brushing and pressing, but all obviously unfitted for the stern task of making Howard Steptoe see reason in the matter of stiff-bosomed shirts for evening wear. If she went back there after lunch, it would, she knew, be merely to inspect a further procession of human rabbits.

Moreover, though now a little subdued by the thought of her coming interview with Mr. Duff, she was a light-hearted girl and enjoyed simple, wholesome comedy. The prospect of watching Mr. Steptoe's reactions, when confronted with Joss, made a strong appeal to her.

"Well, if you're really serious."

"Of course, I'm serious," said Joss. As an alternative to having this girl pass from his life, he would have accepted office as the Claines Hall scullery maid. When love came to them, the Weatherbys did not count the cost.

"You haven't forgotten what I told you about Mr. Steptoe?"

"Yes, I have. What did you tell me about Mr. Steptoe?"

"He's rather a difficult man."

"Tough, eh?"

"Very tough!"

"I understand. One of these twenty-minute eggs. That's quite all right. To one who has been in the entourage of J. B. Duff, all other eggs seem ludicrously soft-boiled. Steptoe will be a nice rest. Well, now that's that settled, how about a bite of lunch?"

"I can't, I'm afraid. I must see Mr. Duff."

"Of course, yes. I was forgetting. I'll send him in."

Mr. Duff was leaning against the wall in a daydream. There had

just floated into his mind like a drifting thistledown the thought
of how pleasant it would be to skin Joss.

"Hey!" said Joss. "You're to go in."

"Well, don't forget you're fired," said Mr. Duff, who wished
to leave no loophole for misunderstanding on this point.

★ 5 ★

As Mr. Duff came into the office and she realized that the fateful interview was about to begin, Sally gave a quick gasp, as if iced water had been poured down her back. She felt like a very small Christian in the arena watching the approach of an outsize lion.

Then, as he advanced and she was able to see him steadily and see him whole, her nervousness left her, giving place to a maternal tenderness. J. B. Duff's features were working in what had the appearance of agony.

The fact was that Mr. Duff, a devil of a fellow among his own sex, was terrified of women. He avoided them if possible, and when cornered by one without hope of escape always adopted the shrewd tactics of the caterpillar of the puss moth—which, we are told by an eminent authority, "not satisfied with Nature's provisions for its safety, makes faces at young birds and alarms them considerably." That was why Mr. Duff's features were working. Nature, making provision for his safety, had given him bushy eyebrows and piercing eyes, and he threw in the faces an an extra.

But to Sally he seemed in pain, and being a nice girl she became the little mother.

"Won't you have some sherry?" she said, remembering what a tonic it had been to her.

This hospitable offer, coming on top of all the other disturbing events of the morning, had the effect of unmanning Mr. Duff for a moment. But he was practical. You have to be, to build up a world-famous hammery. He needed sherry, so he accepted it.

"Thanks," he said gruffly.

"Drink that, and you'll feel better."

"How do you know I'm not feeling fine?"

"I thought Mr. Weatherby might have upset you."

"Young thug!"

"I liked him."

"You can have him."

36

"He's funny."

"He doesn't amuse me."

"Who is he?"

"Look," said Mr. Duff, whom this topic of conversation was afflicting with a rising nausea. "Suppose we don't talk about him any more." It occurred to him that he had not yet been informed to what he owed the honour of this visit. "Who are you?"

"My name is Fairmile."

"You want to see me?"

"Yes."

"What about?"

Sally took the plunge.

"Lord Holbeton asked me to come and see you. I . . . He . . . He's staying at the house where I live."

"Where's that? I haven't heard from him in months. Began to hope he was dead."

A coldness crept into Sally's manner. She decided that she had been wrong in thinking this man an old pet.

"Claines Hall," she said curtly. "It's in Sussex."

"Claines Hall? That's curious. Do you know Mrs. Chavender?"

"Of course."

"Seen that portrait of her that's there?"

"Of course."

"What's it like?"

"It's good."

"It really gets that snooty expression of hers?"

"Oh, yes."

Mr. Duff sighed wistfully.

"But who told you about it?"

"Young Weatherby. He painted it."

"Is he an artist?"

"Yes."

"I was wondering what he was."

"I could tell you what I think he is."

"He must be very clever."

"Now we're back to him again!" said Mr. Duff disgustedly. "I thought you told me you had come to talk about George Trotter."

"George Holbeton."

"Well, George Holbeton, if you prefer it. His father was Percy

Trotter till he started going around under an alias. I suppose he sent you to try to get money out of me?"

"Yes," said Sally, startled at this clairvoyance.

"Why didn't he come himself?"

It was a question which Sally had anticipated.

"He isn't well."

"What's the matter with him?"

"He—er—he's got a sore throat."

"I don't wonder. Does he still sing all the time?"

"He sings quite a lot."

"If you can call it singing. Sounds like gas escaping from a pipe. 'But only God can make a tree.' Bah! In a really civilized community crooners would be shot on sight. Well, I won't give him a penny. How do you come to be mixing yourself up in this?"

"We're engaged."

"What! You've gone and got engaged to George Holbeton?"

"Yes."

"Then you ought to have your head examined," said Mr. Duff. Sally stiffened. Her manner became colder.

"I'm sorry now," she said, "that I gave you that sherry."

"What do you mean, gave me that sherry?" retorted Mr. Duff warmly. "It's my sherry."

The point was one which Sally had overlooked, and she found herself unable to frame a telling reply.

"Engaged to George Holbeton?" said Mr. Duff, marvelling. An idea seemed to strike him. "Are you rich?"

"No."

"Then how on earth can you be engaged to George Holbeton?" said Mr. Duff, plainly bewildered.

"I think I'll go," said Sally.

It seemed that Mr. Duff was quite willing that she should do so. He allowed her to reach the door without speaking. Then suddenly, as her fingers were on the handle, there passed through his portly frame a sort of spasm, causing it to quiver like a jelly. He had the appearance of a man whose brow a thought had flushed.

"Wait!" he cried.

Sally paused, cold and hostile. Her nose was small, but she tilted it with an almost Chavenderesque *hauteur*.

"Why? I've said all I came to say."

"I've a proposition I'd like to put to you."

"You've refused to give George his money."

"Yes, but I think we can do a deal."

"What do you mean?"

"Come and sit down."

Sally returned to her seat.

"Well?"

Mr. Duff was frowning at the desk, as if wondering how to begin. His eye fell on the picture of himself which Joss had drawn for Mrs. Chavender, and he stared at it unpleasantly for a moment. Then he crumpled it up and threw it in the wastepaper basket. The action seemed to have the effect of clearing his mind. He had found the right approach, and in a business conference the right approach is everything.

"Listen," he said. "Lemme tell you a little story."

✭ 6 ✭

SINCE early morning the summer sun had been shining down from a cloudless sky on Claines Hall and neighbourhood. Birds had twittered, bees buzzed and insects tootled. But despite these agreeable weather conditions, the day had been for George, second Baron Holbeton, one of gloom and mental unrest. The strain of waiting for news from the front had brought him within measurable distance of a fit of the vapours.

Mrs. Steptoe's announcement during luncheon that Mr. Duff had been on the telephone, offering extravagant sums for the portrait of Mrs. Chavender, had done nothing to diminish his anxiety. Seeming as it did to indicate that the custodian of his affairs had gone definitely off his onion, it caused him to fear the worst. It is hard enough to get money out of a sane trustee. Let loopiness set in, and the difficulties become immeasurably enhanced.

All through the afternoon his agitation increased. Unaware of the numerous commissions which Mrs. Steptoe had given Sally to execute in the metropolis, he could not understand why she did not appear. By half-past four, as he paced the drive by the main gate, his frame of mind resembled in almost equal proportions that of Mariana in the Moated Grange and of those priests of Baal who gashed themselves with knives.

The sound of a car caused him to spin round with eyes aglow. A natty two-seater was turning in at the gate. Then the glow faded. Its occupant was not Sally but a pleasant-faced young man, a stranger to him, who gave him a genial wave of the hand and passed on towards the house.

The fact that there were suitcases in the rumble seat of the car diverted his thoughts for a while. He had heard of no guest who was expected. Then he dismissed the matter from his mind, and resumed his pacing.

Shadows had begun to creep across the drive before Sally made her appearance. She found him querulous.

"At last!"

"Were you expecting me earlier?"

"Of course I was."

"I had a lot to do."

There was a gaiety in her manner which suddenly caused his spitits to rise. Hope began to dawn. No girl, he reasoned, who had recently got the bird from a provision merchant could be as chirpy as this.

"Well?"

"It's all right."

"You got the money?"

"Not exactly."

"How do you mean?"

"He didn't actually give it to me."

"He's sending it?"

"No. But it's all right. I'd better tell you what happened."

"Yes," said Lord Holbeton, who was anxious to know.

Sally looked about her. Her manner seemed to Lord Holbeton furtive.

"Do you think anyone can hear us?"

"No."

"They might. Get in, and we'll drive along the road."

"What's all the bally mystery about?"

"You'll understand."

She backed the car, and they drove in the direction of Loose Chippings. At the corner by Higgins's duck pond, where there is open country and no facilities for eavesdropping, she halted.

"I've had the weirdest day, George. I met the most extraordinary young man."

Lord Holbeton was not interested in extraordinary young men.

"What happened when you saw old Duff?

"Well, he started by being very rude. I don't think he likes you much."

"He doesn't like anybody."

"Doesn't he? You little know!"

"What do you mean?"

"Though 'like' isn't the right word. Not nearly strong enough. Well, as I say, he started by being very rude. In fact, I was just sweeping out of the room with my nose in the air, when he suddenly said 'Wait!' So I waited."

"And then?"

"He sat waggling his eyebrows for a while, and then he said: 'Let me tell you a little story.'"

"Yes?"

"Well, then he told me it. He said that years ago he had been a young fellow chock-full of romance, and he used to dream all the time of some sweet girl who would come into his life like a tender goddess——"

Lord Holbeton was staring blankly.

"Old Duff said that?"

"Yes."

"You're sure it *was* old Duff?"

"Of course."

"He must have been tight."

"Not a bit, though we had been quaffing sherry. As a matter of fact, sherry flowed like water all the time. Mr. Weatherby found it in a cupboard."

"Who the dickens is Mr. Weatherby?"

"He's the extraordinary young man I told you about. He's done the craziest thing——"

Lord Holbeton's lack of interest in extraordinary young men extended to their unbalanced actions.

"Well, go on. What about my money?"

"Where was I? Oh, yes, about Mr. Duff dreaming of this girl who would come into his life. Well, she came. But unfortunately they quarrelled and she went right out again. And he still loves her! After fifteen years, George. It was the most pathetic thing I ever heard. That poor, lonely old man. My heart just bled for him. Buckets. You know who she is, of course?"

"How on earth should I know?"

"Of course you do. You heard what she was saying at breakfast about having been engaged to him. Mrs. Chavender."

"Oh?" said Lord Holbeton. Except for the fact that this had cleared up the mystery of why Mr. Duff wanted Mrs. Chavender's portrait, he found little in it to interest him. If he had a fault, it was that he was a little self-centred. "Well, how about my money?"

"I'm coming to that. I've got to tell you the whole story, or you won't understand. Mr. Duff still loves Mrs. Chavender. You've got that? Well, he's found out about that portrait of her in the breakfast-room and he's dying to have it. He says he wants to hang it up and gaze at it and think of the old days. So he telephoned Mrs. Steptoe and asked her to sell it to him."

"And about my money?"

"Of course, she refused. Mrs. Chavender gave Mr. Steptoe the portrait, and Mrs. Steptoe wouldn't dare sell it for fear of offending her. Mr. Duff was broken-hearted."

"What did he say about my money?"

"His voice trembled as he told me."

Her own voice trembled. In any girl who is capable of falling beneath the spell of a man who sings *Trees* there must of necessity be a strong vein of sentiment, and J. B. Duff's desire to possess a concrete reminder of the dear old days had affected Sally deeply.

"And then he took my breath away. Do you know what he said?"

"About my money?"

"No, about this portrait. He said he had got to have it somehow. He just had to, he said. And when I said I was afraid I didn't see how it was to be managed, he said you would steal it for him."

A sound like the wind going out of a dying duck escaped Lord Holbeton.

"Steal it?"

"And I said: 'Why, Mr. Duff! What a splendid idea!' "

Lord Holbeton swallowed.

"You said: 'What a splendid idea!'?"

"Yes. Because, you see, he says he will give you your money if you do. And it will be quite easy, he pointed out. He said he wasn't asking you to break into the strong room of the Bank of England and get away with a ton of gold bars. All you will have to do is wait till there's no one about and snip it out of its frame and hide it under your coat."

"Oh?" said Lord Holbeton. He was aware that the remark was a weak one, but at the moment he could think of nothing better.

"One thing I was very firm about, though. His idea was that you should take the thing to him in London, and I absolutely refused to dream of it. I said you were very highly strung and that I wasn't going to have you subjected to any nervous strain. So we left it that he was to come and stay at the Rose and Crown in Loose Chippings, and you will take the portrait to him there."

"Oh?" said Lord Holbeton again.

"So now all you've to do is to find a good opportunity. We mustn't fail the poor old man. He's too touching for words. You should have seen his face light up when I said I thought it was a splendid idea."

Lord Holbeton did not speak. It might have been supposed that what kept him silent was horror at finding the ethical standards of provision merchants so low. This, however, was not the case. He had just begun to wonder whether in plighting his troth to a girl who considered it a splendid idea that he should snip portraits out of their frames and hide them under his coat he might not have acted a little rashly.

7

THE two-seater which had passed Lord Holbeton in the drive continued its progress towards the house, and a few moments later Chibnall, the butler, brooding in his pantry over tea and buttered toast, was roused from a sombre reverie by the sound of the front door bell.

Chibnall, though of a sedate exterior, was a man of strong passions, and what was causing him to brood was the fact that, looking in at the Rose and Crown that morning for a quick one, he had found his *fiancée*, Vera Pym, flirting with a commercial traveller. She had, indeed, been in the very act of straightening the latter's tie, and the sight had given him an unpleasant shock. This was not the first time he had observed in her conduct a levity which he deplored; and though he had said nothing at the time, merely withdrawing in a rather marked manner, it was his intention before the day was done to write her a pretty nasty note and send it round by the knives-and-boots boy.

The bell reminded him that there are other things in life besides woman's faithlessness. It was Chibnall, the lover, who had sat down to tea and toast, but the individual who rose and wiped the butter from his lips and went and opened the front door was Chibnall, the slave of duty.

"Good afternoon," said the pleasant-faced young man whom he found standing on the mat.

"Good afternoon, sir" said Chibnall.

That there are other ways for a new valet to report to G.H.Q. than by driving up to the front door in a sports model car had not occurred to Joss Weatherby. He was fond of motoring, and his first act on leaving Sally had been to go round to the garage and collect the old machine. The stimulating drive through rural England, which was looking its best on this fine afternoon, together with the still more stimulating thought that he was about to take up his residence beneath the same roof as the girl he loved, had lent a sparkle to his eyes and increased the always rather noticeable affability of his manner.

He looked upon Claines Hall, and found it good. The whole
set-up appealed to him enormously. He liked its mellow walls, its
green lawns, its gay flower-beds, its twittering birds, its buzzing
bees and its tootling insects. And when Chibnall appeared, he
beamed at him as if he loved him like a brother. The butler could
not remember when he had opened door to a sunnier visitor.

"Is Mrs. Steptoe at home?"

"Yes, sir."

"Beautiful day."

"Yes, sir."

"Nice place, this. Tudor, isn't it?"

"Yes, sir."

"You don't happen to know what the bird would be that I met
as I came along the drive, do you? Reddish, with a yellow head."

"No, sir."

"A pity," said Joss. "I liked its looks."

Chibnall descended the steps and removed the suitcases from
the car. Like Lord Holbeton, he found himself puzzled by them,
but it was not for him to comment. In God's good time, no doubt,
all would be explained.

"Oh, thanks."

"I will have your car taken round to the stables, sir."

"Will you really?"

To Joss, in his uplifted mood, this seemed so extraordinarily
decent of the man that he had no hesitation in taking a five-pound
note from his pocket and handing it to him. He was glad that his
successful speculation at the charity gambling place had put him
in a position to be able to do so.

"Why, thank you, sir!" ejaculated Chibnall, and blushed to
think how near he had come to saying, "Coo!" Here, he told
himself, was the real thing in guests. Too many of those who had
enjoyed Mrs. Steptoe's hospitality during his term of office had
been content to discharge their obligations with ten bob and a
bright smile. "It is extremely kind of you, sir."

"Not at all."

"If you would come this way, sir, Mrs. Steptoe is in the drawing-
room."

They proceeded thither, chatting amiably of this and that.

Mrs. Steptoe had gone to the drawing-room not to relax but to
concentrate. She was on the eve of giving her first garden party, a
social event of the greatest importance, certain to have wide

repercussions in the County, and she wanted to go through the lists of guests again. She could not rid herself of an uneasy suspicion that she had left out somebody of substance, whose reaction to the slight would be like that of the Bad Fairy who was not invited to the royal christening. Nothing, she knew, more surely gives an aspiring newcomer a social black eye in English County circles than the omission to include in her tea-and-strawberries beano the big shot of the neighbourhood.

Chibnall's smooth "Mr. Weatherby" from the doorway told her how well-founded her fears had been. There was nobody of that name among the "W's," and the quiet distinction of Joss's costume and the carefree jauntiness of his manner made it plain that here was the son of some noble house. And she could not ask him flatly who he was and where he lived, for that way lay the raised eyebrow and the bleak British stare.

She was too forceful a woman actually to flutter, but her voice as she addressed him distinctly shook.

"Oh, how do you do?"

"How do you do?"

"What a lovely day!"

"Delightful."

"So nice of you to call. Do sit down."

She motioned her visitor to a chair, and resumed her own. She was conscious that this was not going to be easy.

The curse of English life, the thing about it that makes strangers put straws in their hair and pick at the coverlet is, of course, the fact that the best type of father so often has sons with totally different names. You get the Earl of Thingummy, for instance. Right. So far, so good. But his heir is Lord Whoosis, and if his union has been still further blessed, the result will be anything from the Hon. Algernon Whatsit to the Hon. Lionel Umph. To ascertain this young man's identity, so that he could be bidden to the garden party, Mrs. Steptoe realized that she might have to uncover layer after layer of nomenclature, like a dancer removing the seven veils.

"Have you come far?" she asked, feeling that here might be a clue on which she could work.

"From London."

"Oh?" said Mrs. Steptoe, baffled.

There was a pause. Joss looked about him, admiring the cosy opulence of his surroundings. A man, he felt, might make himself very snug in a place like this. The reflection that during his stay at Claines Hall he was not likely to be given the run of the drawing-room had not yet suggested itself.

"It must have been warm in London to-day."

"There were moments when things got very warm."

"So pleasant getting back to the country."

"Oh, most."

"Sussex is so lovely at this time of year."

"At any time of year."

"Which part of it do you like best?" asked Mrs. Steptoe, hoping for an outburst of local patriotism.

"All of it. Hullo," said Joss, whose eye, roving along the opposite wall, had been suddenly arrested, "isn't that a Corot over there?"

"I beg your pardon?"

"That picture," said Joss, rising. "A Corot, surely?"

"Is it?" said Mrs. Steptoe, who was not really an authority on art, though she knew what she liked.

"Yes, that's right. His Italian period. Very plastic."

"Oh, yes?"

"Very, ve-ry plastic. I like the structure. Interesting. Calmly stated. Strong, but not bombastic. The values are close, and the colours finely related."

"Perhaps you would care for a cup of tea?" said Mrs. Steptoe.

It may have been a slight asperity in her tone that gave him the feeling, but there came over Joss at this point a sense of something being wrong. Though nothing could have been more enjoyable than this exchange of views on the Barbizon school, he was conscious that in some way he had been remiss. And then he saw what had happened. He had allowed *joie de vivre* to impair his technique. It was all very well to love everybody on this happy day, but he must not forget that he was a gentleman's personal gentleman. Long ere this, he should have been scattering "Madams" like birdseed.

"Thank you, Madam," he said, rectifying the error.

Mrs. Steptoe blinked, but came back strongly.

"Tea's one of your English customs I've taken to in a big way," she said. "My husband doesn't like it, but I never miss my cup at five o'clock."

"Indeed, madam?"

"So refreshing."

"Extremely, madam."

Mrs. Steptoe's embarrassment expressed itself in an uneasy titter. She was beginning to feel unequal to the situation. Her residence in Great Britain had done much to put her abreast of the customs of the country—for weeks she had been eating her boiled eggs out of the shell instead of mashed up in a glass, and Howard was never allowed to fasten the bottom button of his waistcoat—but she knew that there were still weak spots in her equipment, and one of these was that she had not yet quite got the hang of English humour. Sometimes she could grab it off the bat, but sometimes—as now—it got past her.

"Is that the latest gag?" she asked, with what she hoped was adequate sprightliness.

"Madam?"

"Yes, calling women that, like men in the old novels saying 'Dear Lady.' It's kind of cute," said Mrs. Steptoe musingly, "but I'n not sure I really like it. It makes you sound as if you were a valet or something."

"I am, madam."

There came to Mrs. Steptoe an unworthy suspicion. Joss still looked like the son of some noble house, but she now found herself regarding him as the son of a noble house who has had a couple.

"I'm afraid you will think me very dumb," she said coldly, "but I don't quite see the joke."

"No joke, madam. I am Mr. Steptoe's new valet."

"What!"

"Yes, madam. Miss Fairmile engaged me this morning."

There is no anguish so acute as that experienced by a woman of strong views on class distinctions, who, having lavished all the charm of her best manner on a supposed scion of the nobility, discovers that he is the latest addition to her domestic staff. And Mrs. Steptoe would undoubtedly have given eloquent expression to her feelings, had she not, just as she was about to begin, caught Joss's eye. It was a strong, steady eye, the eye of a man who for two years had given J. B. Duff look for look, and if not actually made him wilt at least confined him reasonably closely to the decencies of debate. It impressed Mrs. Steptoe. She could recognize personality when she saw it.

Hard, keen practical woman though she was, the chatelaine of Claines Hall had a wistful, castles-in-the-air building side to her nature. Ever since she had landed in England, she had dreamed of one day securing a valet of the right sort, a gentleman's personal gentleman of blood and iron, capable of sticking his chin out at her Howard and making him play ball. And here, unless she had been totally deceived by a promising exterior, he was.

Her glance softened. An instant before, she could have been mistaken for a rattlesnake about to strike. Her air now became that of a rattlesnake which is prepared to reserve its judgment till it has heard all the facts.

"Oh?" she said.

"Yes, madam."

"Chibnall should have taken you to the servants' hall."

"Yes, madam."

"Still, now you are here——"

"Precisely, madam. No doubt you wish to give me certain hints and instructions with regard to my duties." Joss coughed discreetly. "I understand from Miss Fairmile, madam, that Mr. Steptoe is inclined to be a little difficult."

It was the very point which Mrs. Steptoe was anxious to discuss.

"That's right," she said. "He gets rough with his valets."

"Indeed, madam?"

"He throws a scare into them, and they quit. The only one so far that's stayed as long as two weeks was the fellow before you. I had hopes of him, but Mr. Steptoe finally got him down. He didn't like Mr. Steptoe rubbing his nose on his shirt-front."

This interested Joss. He had not known that he was taking service under a man with an india-rubber neck.

"Is Mr. Steptoe a contortionist?"

"You don't get me. It was the fellow before you's nose that Mr. Steptoe rubbed on Mr. Steptoe's shirt-front. The fellow before you had laid out a stiff-bosomed shirt for him to wear at dinner, and Mr. Steptoe doesn't like stiff-bosomed shirts. So he rubbed the fellow before you's nose on it."

"I see, madam."

"So there you are. That's what you're up against."

"I quite appreciate the situation madam. But I view it without concern. This will not be the first time I have been in the employment of a difficult gentleman."

"And you made out all right?"

"Entirely satisfactorily, madam."

Mrs. Steptoe's last lingering doubts were removed. If she still bore any resemblance to a rattlesnake, it was to one which has heard the voice of conscience and decided to simmer down and spend a quiet evening with the boys. This was the superman she had dreamed of. She resolved to conceal nothing from him, but to give him the low-down in overflowing measure.

"Well, that's fine," she said, "You've taken a weight off my mind. I'm beginning to think you'll be able to swing this job. It's not everybody that can handle Mr. Steptoe when he's going good, but you seem to have what it takes. You see, the whole trouble is this. Mind you, this is strictly off the record. I wouldn't want to be quoted."

"I quite understand, madam."

"Between ourselves, then, for your guidance, Mr. Steptoe is a hick."

"Indeed, madam?"

"He has no natural sense of dignity. I can't seem to drive it into his nut that he's got a position to keep up. Only the other day I caught him in the stable yard, shooting craps with my chauffeur."

"Tut, madam."

"Yes. I heard a voice yelling 'Baby needs new shoes!' and there he was."

"Dear, dear, madam."

"And he hates dressing for dinner. He says collars scratch his neck and he can't stand for the way stiff-bosomed shirts go pop when he breathes. You see, he was raised all wrong. Till I married him, the only time he ever saw a stiff-bosomed shirt was when the referee was bending over him, counting ten."

"Mr. Steptoe was a boxer?"

"Preliminary bouts on the Pacific coast. The first time I ever saw him was at the American Legion stadium in Hollywood. He was getting the tar whaled out of him by a fellow called Wildcat Wix."

This relieved Joss somewhat. He was prepared to take the rough with the smooth, but it was nice to feel that he was not coming up against an irritable world's champion.

"Well, you know what small-time box-fighters are. They get the pork-and-beans outlook, and don't seem able to shake it off. So I'm relying on you to be very firm with him. To-night, particularly. There's one or two really nice people expected to dinner, and I wouldn't put it past Mr. Steptoe, if left to his own unbridled instincts, to show up in a turtleneck sweater. And now I'll ring for Chibnall to take you to your room. I hope you'll be comfortable."

"Thank you, madam."

"Watch Mr. Steptoe's shoes. Take your eye off him for a second, and he'll be coming down to dinner in sneakers."

"I will be very vigilant, madam."

"I'm sure you will. Oh, Chibnall," said Mrs. Steptoe, "this is Weatherby, Mr. Steptoe's new valet. Will you show him his room?"

In stating that there is no anguish so acute as that which is experienced by a hostess who mistakes a member of her staff for a scion of the nobility, we were guilty of an error. It is equalled, if not surpassed, by that of a butler of haughty spirit who finds that he has been calling a fellow-toiler "Sir." It was with burning eyes and resentment in every feature that Chibnall turned on Joss as the door closed behind them. Only the fact that Joss's five-pound note was nestling in his trouser-pocket restrained him from the most violent form of rebuke.

"Why didn't you tell me who you were?" he demanded.

"You never asked me," said Joss.

"Bowling up to the front door in your car, as if you had bought the place!"

"The wrong note, you think? Yes, I suppose you're right. Here, where are we going?"

"I was instructed to show your lordship your lordship's room," said Chibnall, whose satire, though good, was always inclined to be a little on the heavy side. "Perhaps your lordship will be so obliging as to pick up your lordship's feet and follow me."

They had left behind the soft rugs and Chippendale furniture of the ruling classes and had come into a barren land of uncarpeted stairs and passages smelling of yellow soap. Joss found his spirits sinking. He felt like Dante being shown through the Inferno by Virgil. And when Virgil threw open a door in the very heart of the yellow soap zone, revealing a small bedroom with an iron bedstead and a cracked pitcher, standing in a chipped bowl, he shook his head decidedly.

"Oh, no, no, no," he said. "Oh, no, no, no, no, no."

"I beg your pardon?"

"This will never do. Haven't you something better than this?"

"Perhaps you'd like a private bath?"

"A private bath, of course," said Joss. "And a few good prints on the walls and a decent arm-chair. Two arm-chairs, in fact, because I am hoping that you will often look in on me for a smoke and a chat, when we are off duty."

A sharp, whistling intake of breath at his side told him that he had been too abrupt. He felt that he should have remembered that preliminaries are essential to these negotiations.

"I wonder," he said, taking a five-pound note from his pocket, "if you would be interested in another of these? Perhaps you are a collector?"

There was a long pause, during which Chibnall, the man, wrestled with Chibnall the butler. The man wished to fling the five-pound note in Joss's face, the butler was in favour of trousering it. The latter won.

"Thanks," he said.

"You see," Joss explained, "Mrs. Steptoe made such a point of telling me to be comfortable. I wouldn't like to disappoint her. And I ought to tell you that I have not always been as you see me now. Until recently I lived in an atmosphere of refinement, even luxury. In fact, I dwelt in marble halls with vassals and serfs at my side. I can't mention names, even to you, but if I were to reveal the identity of the titled father who cut me off with a shilling for refusing to marry the girl he had chosen for me, you would be staggered."

It was as if Chibnall had suddenly seen light in the darkness. Subconsciously, he realized now, some such explanation of these peculiar goings-on had already begun to suggest itself. He was a great reader of novelettes, and had often argued their merits with Miss Pym, who preferred thrillers. The situation which Joss had outlined was not a new one to him. He had come across it not only in *Hyacinth*, but in *Mark Delamere, Gentleman*, and *The World Well Lost*.

"Indeed, sir?"

"That's what makes me a little fussy."

"I quite understand, sir."

"Who arranges about the bedrooms here?"

"The housekeeper, sir."

"She should be able to find me something suitable?"

"Unquestionably, sir. There are a number of unoccupied guest-rooms."

"Then lead me to her. In fact, you had better assemble the

whole staff. I should like to address them on an important point of policy."

It was some half-hour later, as Joss sat in the servants' hall enjoying a pleasant rubber of bridge with Mrs. Barlow, the housekeeper, Mrs. Ellis, the cook, and Chibnall that there pealed through the regions below stairs the sound of a bell. It gave the impression that somebody with a powerful thumb had placed that thumb on the button and kept it there.

"Mr. Steptoe," said Chibnall, who was dummy.

Joss sighed. Enthusiastically supported by his partner, he had just bid little slam in hearts, and looked like making it.

"A nuisance," he said. "But inevitable, I suppose. Perhaps you would come and show me the way."

The door of Mr. Steptoe's bedroom, when they reached it, was ajar, and from within there came the restless movement of some heavy body, suggesting either that an elephant had got loose or that Mr. Steptoe was pacing the floor. It was a sinister sound, and Chibnall's eyes, as they met Joss's, were alive with respectful pity. Chibnall had seen so many valets enter that room, only to totter out shaking in every limb and groping their way blindly, like guests coming away from a Lord Mayor's Banquet—or even, as in the case of the fellow-before-you, bleeding profusely at the nose.

Quickly shaking Joss's hand, he tiptoed off.

Joss pushed the door open, and went in. It seemed to him that the early stages of his first interview with his new employer might be marked by a little friction. Nor was he mistaken. One glance at the latter was enough to show him that Mr. Steptoe was not at his sunniest.

As a matter of fact, nobody who had known him only since his arrival in England had ever seen Howard Steptoe sunny. He was, as has already been indicated by his demeanour at the breakfast table, a soured and disillusioned man.

When a wealthy widow, infatuated by his robust charms, had removed him from the pork-and-beans surroundings in which he had passed his formative years, Howard "Mugsy" Steptoe had supposed that he was about to sit on top of the world. And here he was in a hell of valets, starched collars, tea parties, County society and companions who were so good for him, like Lord Holbeton. A rude awakening.

To-day, he had been hotting up ever since lunch. It was over the luncheon table, it will be remembered, that Mrs. Steptoe had told him of Mr. Duff's offer for the portrait of Mrs. Chavender. And when a man, sorely in need of ready cash, hears that his wife has turned down a dazzling offer for a portrait, belonging to himself, on which he would have put an outside price of thirty cents, he is apt, even if of a mild and equable temperament, to chafe pretty considerably. Mr. Steptoe, who was not mild and equable, had chafed like a gumboil.

And about half an hour ago he had met Sally and learned from her that a new valet had arrived at Claines Hall. Just when he had been congratulating himself on having stamped this evil out.

Howard Steptoe was waiting for this valet.

"Good evening, sir," said Joss. "You rang?"

He found himself impressed by the other's physique, and was surprised that it had never carried him beyond preliminary bouts on the Pacific coast. Faulty footwork, he presumed.

There was a snowy shirt lying on the bed. Mr. Steptoe pointed a banana-like finger at it—emotionally, for it represented to him the last straw.

"You!"

"Sir?"

"See that shirt?"

"Yes, sir."

"Stiff."

"Precisely, sir."

"Well, take it away, or I'll make you eat it."

Joss felt that the moment had come to be firm. There was a compelling steadiness in the eye which he fixed on the fermenting man.

"Steptoe," he said quietly, "you will wear your nice shirt."

8

THERE was a silence. Mr. Steptoe's vast frame had become afflicted by what looked like a palsy. He moved, he stirred, he seemd to feel the thrill of life along his keel. His hands had bunched themselves into fists, and he breathed tensely through his squashed nose.

"What?" he muttered throatily. "Wassat you said?"

Joss repeated his observation. He had shifted his position slightly, so as to place a substantial chair between them, and had taken from the mantelpiece a stout and serviceable vase—just in case. He was pretty confident of being able to settle this dispute through the channels of diplomacy, but there was no harm in being prepared.

"I'll break you into little bits."

"Don't be silly. What use would I be in little bits?"

A bitter smile disturbed for an instant the tenseness of Mr. Steptoe's lips.

"Ha!" he said. "Smart guy, huh?"

Joss slapped his thigh.

"I knew you were going to say that."

"Is that so?"

"Either that or 'Wise guy, huh? I was as sure of it as I am that I have in my pocket the IOU's for the money you lost to the cook at craps."

"Cheese!" said Mr. Steptoe, tottering on his base.

It was about a week since Howard Steptoe, in the hope of picking up a little pocket-money, had started teaching the domestic staff this fascinating game, and in a black hour had come up against Mrs. Ellis, the cook, who possessed a natural aptitude for it. This very evening he had been compelled to ask her to accept another promissory note for sixteen shillings, bringing his obligations up to the colossal figure of six pounds, eight and twopence.

"And when I think what Mrs. Steptoe is going to say when I show them to her," said Joss, "I shudder."

So did Mr. Steptoe. He shuddered from stem to stern.

The fear lest this evidence of his sinning might some day find its way to Mrs. Steptoe had haunted Mugsy's dreams for a week. He knew so well what the harvest would be.

In the main, though despotic, his wife's rule was benevolent, and the love she bore him enabled him to rub valets' noses in shirt-fronts without exciting anything worse than a pained "Oh, Howard!" She had even been reasonably mild when she had found him rolling the bones with the chauffeur.

But there was one point on which he knew that she would tolerate no funny business. Let her discover that he had been trying to skin the best cook in Sussex, thus sowing in that cook's mind possible thoughts of giving her notice, and the tigress that slept in her would be unchained.

"Anticipating a spot of toughness on your part," said Joss, "I leaped at the opportunity offered to me just now of buying up your paper. It may interest you to know that I got it dirt cheap. Confidence in your financial stability is very low in the servants' hall, and sacrifice prices prevailed." He paused. "Steptoe," he said, "you will wear your stiff-bosomed shirt, and like it."

Mr. Steptoe had sunk into a chair, and was supporting his head on his hands. Joss felt a pang of pity for the stricken man.

"Cheer up," he said. "You have only to show a docile and reasonable spirit, and I shall not proceed to the last awful extreme. How on earth," he asked sympathetically, "did you come to get in the red to that extent? You must have been rolling them all wrong. You'd better let me give you a few lessons."

Mr. Steptoe raised his head, staring.

"Do you play craps?"

"Do I play craps?" said Joss, with a light laugh. "That's good. The dicers of a dozen cities would smile if they heard you ask that. You, I take it, are a novice."

"No, I'm not," said Mr. Steptoe hotly.

"Then there must be something seriously wrong with your methods. The whole science of craps consists in saying the right thing to the bones at the right time. And that, I suspect, is where you have slipped. You suggest to me the ultraconservative, hidebound personality. What you learned at your mother's knee is good enough for you. I understand that you still say 'Baby needs new shoes.' "

"Well, why not?"

"All wrong. Dice aren't going to respond to outmoded stuff like that. But I'll go into all that later. For the moment, Steptoe, let me urge upon you never again to play with cooks. Practically all of them have an uncanny skill. Your future as a crapshooter, as I see it, lies among the nobility and gentry. If I were you, I would reserve myself for this garden party of which I hear so much."

"How do you mean?"

"Wait till the garden party, and then detach a contingent of the best element in the County from the tea and buns and take them behind the stables and give them the works."

"I never thought of that."

"I see no reason why you should not make a substantial killing."

"It can't be too substantial for me."

"You require the money for some special purpose?"

"Do I!" Although they were alone, behind closed doors, Mr. Steptoe looked nervously over his shoulder. "I want to raise enough to buy my transportation back to Hollywood."

"Your heart is still there, is it? But I was given to understand that your career there was not an unmixedly successful one. Suppose you ran into Wildcat Wix again?"

"Say, listen, I could eat that guy for breakfast."

"I was told that he whaled the tar out of you."

"Who said that?"

"Mrs. Steptoe."

"Women don't understand these things. I was robbed of the decision by a venal referee. And, anyway, I'm not planning to go back to being a box-fighter. When I left there, I was doing swell in pictures."

"I don't remember seeing you."

"Well, it was extra work till just at the end. Then I was in one where I had three good speeches."

"You had?"

"That's what I had. It was one of these tough stories, where everybody's all the time slapping somebody else's face. I was one of these gangsters. A guy comes up to me and says 'Oh, yeah?' and I say 'Oh, yeah?' and slap his face. Then another guy comes up to me and says 'Oh, yeah?' and I say 'Oh, yeah?' and slap his face. And then a third guy comes up to me and says 'Oh, yeah?' and I say 'Oh, yeah?' and I slap him on the kisser, too."

"I suppose they couldn't get Clark Gable?"

"And then Mrs. Steptoe goes and marries me. Wouldn't that jar you? Just as I'm starting to break in."

"Many people say that the artist should not marry."

"It bust my career. There's a rising demand in pictures for fellows with maps like mine. Look at Wallace Beery. Look at Edward G. Robinson. How about Maxie Rosenbloom? There's a case for you. Started out as a box-fighter, like me, and now look at him."

"Maxie was a champion."

"Well, so would I of been a champion if it hadn't of been for jealousy in high places. I tell you, I was being groomed for stardom when Mrs. Steptoe comes along and takes me away from it all. And all that stands between me and it now is not having the dough for my transportation."

"A lesson or two from me, and we'll soon adjust that. You'll send those Dukes and Earls back from the garden party in their shirts."

"I cert'ny will. Say, listen," said Mr. Steptoe, regarding Joss with affection and respect. "You're all right!"

"I'm one of the nicest fellows you ever met. In proof of which, take these."

"Cheese!"

"I merely needed them at the outset of our acquaintance to ensure the establishing of our relations on a chummy basis. And now," said Joss briskly, "as time is getting on, climb into that shirt."

The joyous light died out of the other's eyes.

"Must I?"

"I'm afraid so. People are coming to dinner."

"Just a bunch of stiffs."

"The stiffer the stiffs, the stiffer the shirt-front. That is the fundamental law on which Society rests. So upsy-daisy, Steptoe, and get it over."

"Well, if you say so."

"That's my brave little man. And now," said Joss, who had been looking out of the window, "I must leave you. There's somebody down in the garden that I want to see."

9

SALLY had dressed for dinner early, in order to be able to enjoy a stroll in the garden before the guests should arrive. Claines Hall was one of the moated houses of England, and a walk beside those still waters always refreshed her after one of her visits to London.

Her thoughts, as she leaned over the low wall, looking down at the fish darting in and out of the weeds, had turned to Joss. As his social sponsor, she felt herself concerned in his fortunes. She wondered how he was settling down in the servants' hall, and hoped that that exuberance of his had not led him into the perpetration of one of those *gaffes* which are so rightly resented in such places.

It was nice, at any rate, to find that he had been an outstanding success with Mrs. Steptoe. That autocrat's enthusiastic response to her rather apprehensive enquiries had astonished Sally. Mrs. Steptoe had unhesitatingly stamped Joss with the seal of her approval as the goods. She had spoken in no measured terms of the quiet forcefulness of his personality, giving it as her opinion that this time the master of the house had come up against something red-hot. If his new fellow was as good as he seemed, said Mrs. Steptoe, not mincing her words, it was quite within the bounds of possibility that Howard might make his appearance at the garden party looking half-way human.

A cheery "Hoy!" broke the stillness, and she turned to see the very person she had been thinking about. Valets did not as a rule saunter about the gardens of Claines Hall in the quiet evenfall, but nobody had told Joss Weatherby that.

"So there you are," he said. "Do you know, in this uncertain light I mistook you for a wood nymph."

"Do you always shout 'Hoy!' at wood nymphs?"

"Nearly always."

"I suppose you know that valets aren't supposed to shout 'Hoy!' at people?"

"You must open a conversation somehow."

"Well, if you want to attract, for instance, Mrs. Steptoe's attention, it would be more suitable to say 'Hoy, madam.' "

"Or 'Hoy, dear lady!' "

"Yes, that would be friendlier."

"Thanks. I'll remember it." He joined her at the wall, and stood scrutinizing the fish for a moment in silence. The evening was very still. Somewhere in the distance, sheep bells were tinkling, and from one of the windows of the house there came the sound of a raucous voice rendering the Lambeth Walk. Despite the shirt, Joss had left Mr. Steptoe happy, even gay. "This is a lovely place," he said.

"I'm glad you like it."

"An earthly Paradise, absolutely. Though mark you," said Joss, who believed in coming to the point, " a gas works in Jersey City would be all right with me, so long as you were there. A book of verses underneath the bough——"

The quotation was familiar to Sally, and she felt it might be better to change the subject.

"How are you getting on?"

"Fine. Couldn't be better. I was hoping to run across you, and here you are. And as I was saying, a jug of wine, a loaf of bread and thou beside me, singing in the wilderness——"

"I didn't mean in the wilderness. I meant in the servants' hall."

"Oh, the servants' hall? I'm its pet."

"Chibnall, of course, is the man you have to conciliate. His word can make or break."

"I have Chibnall in my pocket."

"Really?"

"We're like Cohen and Corcoran. One of those beautiful friendships. We hadn't known each other half an hour before he was taking his hair down and confiding in me. Did you know he was engaged to the barmaid at the local pub?"

"No."

"Perhaps it hasn't been given out yet. And he was a good deal upset because he found her this morning straightening a commercial traveller's tie. Oh curse of marriage, he said to himself, that we can call these delicate creatures ours, but not their appetites. His impulse was to write her a stinker."

"And did you approve?"

"No. I was against it. I pointed out to him that it is of the essence of a barmaid's duties that she be all things to all men, and that it had probably been a mere professional gesture, designed purely to stimulate trade. I am a close enough student of human nature to be aware that a commercial traveller who has had his tie straightened by a pretty girl with copper-coloured hair is far more likely to order a second beer than one to whom such girl has been distant and aloof."

"That's true. He must have found you a great comfort."

"Oh, he did. He's going to introduce me to her to-morrow."

"You seemed to have comforted Mr. Steptoe, too. That sounds like him singing."

"Yes. I found him rather moody, but I dropped a few kindly words, and they cheered him up like a noggin of J. B. Duff's sherry. I forgot to ask about that, by the way. Did you and he finish the bottle after I had left ?"

"Not quite."

"Was the interview satisfactory ?"

"Very, thanks."

"Let me see, I forget what it was you were seeing him about?"

"You should take one of these memory courses. How do you get on with the others?"

"They eat out of my hand."

"Has Mrs. Barlow given you a nice room?"

"Terrific."

"Then you think you will be happy here?"

"Ecstatically."

"How are you going to manage about looking after Mr. Steptoe? Can you valet?"

"You have touched on my secret sorrow. I can't. But it's all arranged. Immediately upon arrival, I summoned the staff and addressed them. I said that if they were prepared to take my work off my hands I was prepared to pay well for good service. I had the meeting with me from the start, and the details were speedily fixed up. Charles, the footman, will see to the technical side of Mr. Steptoe's valeting. The matter of my morning cup of tea is in the capable hands of the kitchen maid. The cook has contracted to see that a few sandwiches shall be beside my bed last thing at night, in case I get peckish in the small hours. The whisky and soda to accompany them will of course be in Chibnall's department."

Sally stared. For one disloyal moment she found herself regretting that Lord Holbeton had not more of this spirit of enterprise. It might have been purely her fancy, but she thought she had detected in the latter's manner, when she broached the idea of stealing Mrs. Chavender's portrait, a certain listlessness and lack of enthusiasm.

"You're quite an organizer."

"I like to get things working smoothly."

"What used you to be before this? A captain of industry? But I was forgetting. Mr. Duff said you were an artist."

"Yes."

"Then what were you doing in his office? When I came in, I thought you must be a partner or something."

"That is a mistake lots of people used to make. My air of quiet dignity was misleading. I was a kind of tame artist employed by the firm to do illustrations for advertisements and so on. Among other things, I did the posters for Paramount Ham."

"Oh, no!"

"All right, I don't like them myself."

"But Mr. Duff told me you painted that portrait of Mrs. Chavender that's in the breakfast-room."

"Quite true."

"Then why——?"

"The whole trouble was," said Joss, "that the necessity for eating thrust itself into the foreground of my domestic politics. When I painted that portrait, I was in the chips. I had a private income—the young artist's best friend. It was later converted to his own use by the lawyer who had charge of it, he getting the feeling one day that his need was greater than mine. When you're faced by the pauper's home, you have to take what you can get."

"Yes," said Sally, who had had the same experience. "But what a shame! I'm sorry."

"Thanks," said Joss. "Thanks for being sorry. Well, I struggled along for a while, getting thinner and thinner, and finally did what I ought to have had the sense to do at the start. I saved J. B. Duff from a watery grave. We were at Easthampton at the time, he on his yacht, I holding an executive post in a local soda fountain, and we met in mid-ocean. I got him to shore, and in a natural spasm of gratitude he added me to his London staff. He was just leaving for London, to take charge. I have an idea he has regretted it since. Thinking it over, I believe he wishes occasionally that he had gone down for the third time."

"I can see how you might not be everybody's dream-employee."

"Too affable, you think?"

"A little, perhaps. Well, it's a shame."

"Oh, all in the day's work. Some day I hope to be able to be a portrait painter again. The difficulty is, of course, that in order to paint portraits you have to have sitters, and you can't get sitters till you've made a name, and you can't make a name till you've painted portraits. It is what is known as a vicious circle."

"Very vicious."

"Almost a menace. But let's not waste time talking about me. Let's go on to that dress you're wearing. It's stupendous."

"Thank you."

"It looks as if it were woven of mist and moonbeams. Mist and moonbeams, and you inside. Beat that for a combination. It's a most extraordinary thing. You seem to go from strength to strength. When you came into the office this morning in that blue frock, I thought it was the last word in woman's wear. And now you knock my eye out with this astounding creation. But of course, it isn't the upholstery, it's you. You would look wonderful in anything. Tell me," said Joss, "there's a thing I've been waiting to discuss with you ever since we met. Do you believe in love at first sight?"

Once more, Sally had the feeling that the conversation might be changed.

"The ducks nest on that island over there," she said, pointing at a dim mass that loomed amid the shadows of the moat.

"Let them," said Joss cordially. "Do you?"

"Do I what?"

"Believe in love at first sight. Chibnall does."

A car rounded the corner of the drive, and came raspingly to a halt at the front door.

"I must go," said Sally.

"Oh, no, don't."

"People are arriving."

"Just a bunch of stiffs. I have this on Mr. Steptoe's authority. Pay no attention to them."

"Good night."

"You really are going?"

"Yes."

"Then I shall look forward to seeing you to-morrow, and we will take up this subject where we left off. There was some famous fellow who fell in love at first sight. Not Chibnall. Somebody else. Where do you stroll in the mornings?"

"I don't stroll. I work."

"Work?"

"Yes. I see the cook——"

"Don't take her on at craps."

"And I do the flowers and I brush the dog——"

"I'll help you brush the dog."

"No, you won't."

"Why not?"

"It would excite remark."

"I being a humble valet?"

"You being a humble valet."

"What a curse these social distinctions are. They ought to be abolished. I remember saying that to Karl Marx once, and he thought there might be an idea for a book in it. Romeo! That's the name I was trying to think of."

"What about him?"

"He fell in love at first sight, like Chibnall and——"

"Good night," said Sally.

⋆ 10 ⋆

IT was on a Tuesday that Mr. Duff had conferred with Sally in his office. Wednesday morning found him in the bar parlour of the Rose and Crown, sipping a small gin and ginger.

J. B. Duff was not a man who procrastinated. He thought on his feet and let no grass grow under them. Sally had returned to Claines Hall at half-past four on the previous afternoon, charged with the task of opening negotiations with Lord Holbeton for the removal of Mrs. Chavender's portrait. At seven, Mr. Duff was alighting at Loose Chippings station, all ready to be on the spot the moment anything broke. But one glance out of the window, as his cab rolled up the High Street, had been enough to tell him that this was not the place of his dreams. As he sipped his gin and ginger, he was feeling homesick.

Towns like Loose Chippings (Pop. 4,916) are all right if you are fond of towns with Pops. of 4,916, but Mr. Duff's tastes had always been metropolitan. And now, although it was so brief a time ago that his arrival had made the Pop. 4,917, it seemed to him that he had been here ever since he was a small boy, getting more bored every minute. Like some minstrel of Tin Pan Alley, he was wishing that he could go back, back, back to the place where he was born, which was Greater New York—or, failing that, to his adopted city of London.

There is never a great deal doing in the bar parlour of a country inn at eleven o'clock in the morning. It is only later in the day that it becomes the hub of the neighbourhood's social life, attracting all that is gayest and wittiest for miles around. The only other occupant of the room at this moment was the girl with copper-coloured hair who sat behind the counter reading a mystery story. Vera Pym, barmaid, the affianced of Chibnall, the butler.

The first thing any regular client would have noticed, had he entered, was that Miss Pym was strangely silent. As a rule, when she found herself alone with a customer, she felt it her duty to be the hostess, and it was her practice to chat with great freedom,

66

ranging vivaciously from politics and the weather to darts gossip and the new films. But now she had not spoken for nearly ten minutes. She sat reading her book and from time to time shooting quick, sidelong glances in Mr. Duff's direction. There was nervousness in these glances, and a sort of shocked horror.

This, as we say, would have mystified the regular client. But her taciturnity may be readily explained. What was causing it was the fact that Mr. Duff was wearing on his upper lip a large moustache of the soup-strainer type. It lent to his aspect a strange and rather ghastly menace. Who knew, the observer felt as he saw it, what sinister things might not be lurking within that undergrowth, waiting to spring out and pounce.

That was what Miss Pym was feeling, as she eyed it with those quick, sidelong glances. She had a complex about moustaches. So many of the worst bounders in the crime fiction to which she was addicted had affected them. The mysterious leper and the man with the missing toe were examples that leaped to her mind. In both these instances the shrubbery had proved to be as false as its wearer's heart, and the more she eyed Mr. Duff's, the surer she became that it was not a natural disfigurement but had been stuck on with glue.

It was no idle whim that had led Mr. Duff to bar his features to the general public in this manner. Prudence and foresight had guided his actions. In coming to Loose Chippings, only a stone's throw from the residence of Mrs. Chavender, he had never lost sight of the fact that he was entering a danger zone. At any moment he might run into his old love, and the thought of such an encounter was one that froze the grand old bachelor's blood. False moustaches cost money, but he had considered it money well spent.

He finished his gin and ginger, and got up.

"Say," he said, and Miss Pym leaped like a rising trout. A most impossible outsider, who went about shooting people with a tommy gun, had just said "Say" in the story she was reading.

"Sir?" she faltered.

"How do you get to a place called Claines Hall?"

"Turn to the left as you leave the inn and straight along the road," said Miss Pym faintly.

"Thanks," said Mr. Duff, and making for the door collided with Chibnall, who was entering at the moment, accompanied by Joss.

"Pardon," said Chibnall.

"Grrh," said Mr. Duff.

Joss looked after him, puzzled. Mr. Duff reminded him in an odd sort of way of someone he had met somewhere, possibly in a nightmare. He found himself, however, unable to place him, and came back to the present to find that Chibnall was presenting him to his betrothed.

"Mr. Weatherby is Mr. Steptoe's new personal attendant."

"How do you do, Mr. Weatherby?"

"How do you do?" said Joss. He submitted Miss Pym to a quick inspection, and was able to assure Chibnall with a swift lift of the right eyebrow that in his opinion the other's judgment had been sound. A girl well fitted to be the butler's bride, was Joss's verdict.

Gratified by this, Chibnall talked easily and well, and for some minutes it seemed that a perfect harmony was to prevail. Then he struck what was to prove to be a discordant note.

"Who was the walrus?" he asked, for he was always interested in new faces in the bar parlour.

Miss Pym polished a glass thoughtfully. Her manner, which had been animated, had become grave.

"I've never seen him before."

"I thought I had," said Joss. "His face seemed somehow familiar."

"He's staying at the inn," said Miss Pym. "And if you want to know what I think, Sidney——"

Chibnall laughed amusedly, as one who has heard this before and knows what is coming. To Joss, who had a sensitive ear, it seemed that there was far too strong a note of "Silly little woman" about that laugh, and it was plain that Miss Pym thought so, too, for she bridled visibly.

"All right. You can laugh as much as you like, but if you want to know what I think, I believe he's a crook."

Chibnall laughed again, once more with offensive masculine superiority.

"You and your crooks. What's gone and put that idea into your head?"

"I think it's suspicious, him being at the inn. He's not an artist, he's not a commercial, and he hasn't come for the fishing, because he's not brought any rods and things."

"He may be one of these writers, come down here to work where it's quiet."

"Well, what's he wearing a false moustache for?"

"How do you know it's false?"

"I have a feeling."

"Pooh!"

"Pooh to you!" retorted Miss Pym.

It seemed to Joss that he was becoming involved in a lovers' quarrel. This, and the fact that he had promised to meet Mr. Steptoe in the stable yard at noon and give him a craps lesson, decided him to finish his half of bitter and leave. He excused himself and went out, and Chibnall, lighting a cigarette, took up the discussion where it had been broken off.

"If you want to know what's the matter with you, my girl, you read too many of these trashy detective stories."

"Better than reading silly novelettes."

"May I ask why you call novelettes silly?"

"Because they are."

"Mere abuse is no criticism."

"Well, they're full of things happening that don't happen."

"Such as?"

"Well, what we were talking about the other day. Whoever heard of a young fellow being buzzed out of his home because his father wanted him to marry somebody and he wouldn't?"

Chibnall blew an airy smoke ring. With subtle cunning, he had contrived to work the conversation round to the exact point where he wanted it. His love, deep though it was, had never blinded him to the fact that what the modern young woman needed, for the discipline of her soul, was to be properly scored off and put in her place from time to time.

"You will doubtless be surprised to learn," he said with quiet satisfaction, "that a case of that very nature has come under my own personal notice. I allude to Mr. Weatherby, who has just left us."

"I suppose he's the son of a Duke, who gave him the push for not marrying the girl he had picked out for him?"

"He did not specify a Duke—he merely referred to a titled father—but that, substantially, was the story he told."

"He was pulling your leg."

"Not at all. I had spotted already that he was no ordinary valet. You should have seen him turning up his nose at his room and insisting on something more like what he'd been accustomed to."

"What cheek! Didn't you tell him off?"

"Certainly not. I wouldn't have taken the liberty."

Miss Pym polished a glass, derision in every flick of the cloth.

"And then, of course, he tried to borrow money from you?"

"On the contrary, he tipped me ten pounds. A little more of that sort of thing, and I'll have enough saved to buy that pub I've got my eye on, and we'll be able to put up the banns."

Miss Pym had lowered the glass. There was horror in her eyes.

"Ten pounds?"

"Ten pounds."

"Ten *pounds*?"

"I thought you'd be surprised."

"Surprised? I'm scared stiff. I suppose you know what this fellow is?"

"Is he a crook, too?"

"Of course he is. He must be. Don't you ever go to the pictures? He's one of these gangsters that's just pulled off a big thing and is using the Hall as a hide-out. Where would a chap whose father had bunged him out get ten poundses to tip people with?"

Chibnall frowned. He did not like this feverish imagination of hers. He thought it unwholesome.

"Pooh!" he said.

"Pooh to you!" said Miss Pym. "Oh, well, I don't suppose there's a hope of opening your eyes to the realities of life, but everybody except you knows that that sort of thing is happening all the time. You read your *News of the World*, don't you? You've heard of Mayfair Men, haven't you? But you can talk to some people till you're blue in the face."

"Don't you go getting blue in the face. It wouldn't suit you. Oh, well," said Chibnall, looking at his watch, "back to the old job, I suppose. You'll be round for tea to-morrow?"

The question was purely a perfunctory one. To-morrow was Miss Pym's afternoon off; and on these occasions she always came to his pantry for a cosy cup of tea. To his amazement, she was evasive.

"I'll ring you up."

"How do you mean, ring me up?"

"Just possible," said Miss Pym, who had been deeply piqued by her loved one's scepticism, "that I may be engaged."

The butler froze.

"Oh, very well," he said aloofly "If I'm not in, leave a message."

He stalked out, hurt and offended. As he made his way along the road, all those old doubts which Joss's soothing reasoning had dispelled came back to gnaw at his heart. The image of that commercial traveller rose before his eyes. In speaking of this butler, we must speak of one that loved not wisely but too well; of one not easily jealous, but being wrought perplexed in the extreme. Dark suspicions came flooding in on Sidney Chibnall as he walked, and he writhed freely.

Mr. Duff, meanwhile, was approaching Claines Hall.

In the light of what has been said about his apprehensions concerning a chance meeting with Mrs. Chavender, it might seem that a madness had fallen upon this ham-distributor, robbing him of his usual calm judgment. But he had the situation well in hand. It was not his intention to penetrate to the Hall's front door—he was not so reckless as that—he merely intended to prowl about in the vicinity on the chance of getting a word with Lord Holbeton.

He was intensely anxious to establish contact with that young man at the first possible moment, in order to learn from him how prospects looked for an early delivery of the portrait. The sooner he could get away from the Rose and Crown, whose ecentric cooking had already begun to give him the feeling that sinister things were happening inside him, the better he would be pleased.

The distance from the inn door to the main entrance of the Hall was just under a mile, and he had covered the greater part of it when he perceived that this was his lucky morning. Just ahead of him, turning in at the gate, was the very man he sought. Though not fond of active exercise, he broke into a clumsy gallop, at the same time shouting that favourite word of his—"Hey!"

It was in order to ponder over the future that Lord Holbeton had gone for his solitary walk. He found in this future much food for meditation.

Sally, in assigning to him the task of snipping portraits out their frames in a house where he was an honoured guest, had seemed to take if for granted that he would leap at it without hesitation. He found himself unable to share her sunny enthusiasm.

All crooners are nervous men—the twiddly bits seem to affect their moral stamina—and Lord Holbeton was no exception. Only the reflection of how much he needed the money had enabled him even to contemplate the venture as a possibility. And the more he contemplated it, the less of a possibility did it seem. As he started to walk up the drive, he had just begun to toy with the thought of what would happen if Mrs. Steptoe caught him in the act.

The shout and the sound of pursuing footsteps in his rear came to him, consequently, at a moment when he was not feeling at the peak of his form. He turned, and was aware of a densely moustached stranger galloping up, shouting "Hey!"

The attitude of people towards densely moustached strangers who are galloping up, shouting "Hey!" varies a good deal according to the individual. Joss Weatherby in such circumstances would have stood his ground and investigated the phenomenon. So, probably, would Napoleon, Joe Louis and Attila the Hun. Lord Holbeton was made of more neurotic stuff. The spectacle, acting upon his already enfeebled morale, was too much for him. Directing at the other a single horrified glance, he was off up the drive with a briskness which would have put him immediately out of range of anything that was not a jack rabbit. And even a jack rabbit would have been extended.

J. B. Duff gave up the chase, and came to a halt, panting. He mopped his forehead, and broken words, unworthy of a leading provision merchant, fell from his trembling lips.

He felt profoundly discouraged. He had never thought highly of Lord Holbeton as an agent, and this extraordinary behaviour on his part convinced him that the fellow was a broken reed. Like so many heavily moustached men, Mr. Duff was unaware of the spiritual shock, akin to that experienced by Macbeth on witnessing the approach of the forest of Dunsinane, which the fungus had on nervous persons who saw it suddenly on its way towards them. All he felt was that in hoping that a total loss like the sprinter who had just left him would be capable of the dashing act of purloining the Chavender portrait, he had been guilty of wishful thinking of the worst type.

Yet, failing him, to whom could he look for assistance?

Just when it was that a voice whispered in his ear that homely saw: "If you want a thing well done, do it yourself," he could not have said. One moment, the idea was not there; the next it was, and he was examining it carefully with a growing feeling that he had got something.

It is possible, however, that he might have been unable to screw his courage to the sticking point, had there not come along at this moment from the direction of the house a two-seater car, containing in addition to the very pretty girl at the wheel, in whom he recognized his visitor of yesterday, two passengers, one human, the other canine. Mrs. Chavender's Pekinese, Patricia, had woken up that morning a little below par, and Sally was driving her and it to the veterinary surgeon in Lewes.

Mrs. Chavender gave Mr. Duff an uninterested glance in passing, evidently taking him for just another of the strange fauna which are always drifting up and down the drives of country houses. He, on his side, gasped quickly and reeled a little, like an African explorer who sees a rhinoceros pass by without having had its attention drawn to him. The luck of the Duffs, he felt, was in the ascendant. The coast was now clear, and he could carry on with an easy mind.

Ten minutes later, after one or two false starts, he had located the breakfast-room, and was peering through its open French windows at the fireplace and what hung above it.

Even now, though twenty-four hours had elapsed since they had had their little unpleasantness, Mr. Duff's feelings towards Joss Weatherby were not cordial. The desire to skin him still lingered. But he had to admit that the young hound, in painting that portrait, had done a good job. It was all he had said it was, and more, and it drew Mr. Duff like a magnet. He was inside the room, creeping across the floor like a leopard, when his concentration was disturbed by the falling on his shoulder of a heavy hand, and he found himself gazing into the eyes of an enormous man with a squashed nose and ears that seemed to be set at right angles to his singularly unprepossessing face.

"What's the idea?" enquired this person.

Mr. Duff's heart, which had been dashing about in his mouth like an imprisoned rabbit, returned slowly to its base. He swallowed once or twice, and his moustache trembled gently, like a field of daffodils stirred by a March wind.

"It's all right," he said ingratiatingly.

He had endeavoured to inject into the words all the charm of which he was capable, and it was with a pang that he saw that his effort had been wasted.

"You go spit up a rope," retorted his companion. "It's not all right. What you doing in my house?"

"Are you Mr. Steptoe?"

"I am."

The situation was unquestionably a difficult one, but Mr. Duff persevered.

"Pleased to meet you," he said.

"You won't be long," predicted the other.

"I guess it seems funny to you, finding me here."

"A scream. I'm laughing my head off."

"I can explain everything."

"I'm listening."

"Lemme tell you a little story."

"It better be good."

"My name is Duff."

Mr. Steptoe started. It was plain that the name had touched a chord.

"Duff? The guy that was on the phone yesterday, making an offer for that portrait?"

"That's right."

There was no need for the little story. Mr. Steptoe was not a highly intelligent man, but he could put two and two together.

"Now I got it. So when Mrs. Steptoe turned you down, you think to yourself you'll gumshoe in and swipe the thing?"

"No, no. I—er—just wanted to look at it."

"Oh, yeah?"

"Well, I'll tell you."

"You don't have to. Listen. How bad do you want that portrait?"

"Listen. I've just got to have it. Can you," asked Mr. Duff, his voice trembling emotionally, "understand a man pining for a woman he's loved and lost and wanting to have her portrait so that he can sit and look at it and dream of what might have been?"

"Sure," said Mr. Steptoe cordially. "I've seen somebody doing that in the pictures. I've an idea it was Lionel Barrymore. Either him or Adolph Menjou. I guessed it must be something like that, when Mrs. Steptoe told me about you phoning. Listen. Was it right what she said, that you're willing to pay good money for it?"

"Listen," said Mr. Duff. "The sky's the limit."

"You mean that?"

"Well, within reason," said Mr. Duff, his native prudence jogging his elbow.

"Then let's go," said Mr. Steptoe. "You need the old portrait. I need the old money. Got a knife?"

"No."

"Nor me. I'll go fetch one," said Mr. Steptoe, and bounding to the door checked himself just in time to avoid a collision with the lady of the house. He recovered his balance, which he had lost by tripping over his large feet, a constant habit of his pugilistic days and one which had done much to prevent him rising to great heights in his profession. "Oh, hello, honey," he said, giggling girlishly. "Meet Mr. Duff."

It seemed to Mr. Duff, as it would have seemed to any sensitive man, that at this woman's entrance a chill had crept into the warmth of the summer day. He fingered his moustache nervously.

Mrs. Steptoe's eyes were roaming over his person with a distressing effect on his equanimity. They were at their coldest and hardest. Like her husband, she could put two and two together, and she found no difficulty in accounting for Mr. Duff's presence. He had come, she concluded, to plead in person for the boon which had been denied him over the telephone. Her lips tightened. She disapproved of these follow-up campaigns. When she announced a decision, she liked to have it accepted.

"Duff?"

"I spoke to you on the telephone yesterday, Mrs. Steptoe——"

"Yes. And I have nothing to add to what I said then. The portrait is not for sale. Howard, show Mr. Duff out."

"Yes, honey."

In the aspect of the two men, as they shambled through the French windows, there was a crushed defeatism which would have reminded Napoleon, had he been present, of the old days at Moscow. Neither spoke until they were out of sight and hearing of the room they had left. Then Mr. Steptoe producing a handkerchief, and passing it over his brow, said "Cheese!" adding the words: "No dice!"

"Brother," he went on, clarifying his meaning beyond all chance of misunderstanding, "it's off!"

"What!"

"It's cold."

"You mean you won't get it?"

"I haven't the nerve."

"Think of the money," pleaded Mr. Duff.

Mr. Steptoe was thinking of the money, and it was as if wild cats were clawing his vitals. His face was drawn with anguish.

Then, abruptly, it brightened, and Mr. Duff, startled by his sudden look of animation, wondered what had caused it. It seemed absurd to suppose that the other had had an idea, yet something was unmistakably stirring behind that concrete brow.

"Oi!" cried Mr. Steptoe.

"Yes?" said Mr. Duff. "Yes?"

"Listen. What's that thing fellows have to have? You know, when they're up against a stiff proposition and get cold feet."

"Grit?"

"Something to give them grit. Moral support! That's it. If I'm to put this deal through, I got to have moral support. And I know where to get it. My new valet. We'll bring him in on this."

"Your valet?"

"Wait, till you see him. He's a wonder. Come along to the stable yard and we'll put it up to him. He's waiting there to give me a craps lesson."

Joss was not only waiting, but getting tired of waiting. He was, indeed, on the point of giving his pupil up and leaving in dudgeon, when he observed him approaching. And with him, he saw with surprise, was the moustached stranger of the inn who had reminded him of something he had seen in a nightmare.

And now that the latter was close enough to be examined in detail, recognition came.

"J.B.!"

"Weatherby!"

"Well, for Pete's sake," said Mr. Steptoe, marvelling. "Do you guys know each other?"

"Do we know each other?" said Joss. "Why, I look on J. B. Duff as a grandfather. Who ran to catch me when I fell, and would some pretty story tell and kiss the place to make it well? J. B. Duff."

"Well, say, that's swell," said Mr. Steptoe. "If you're that way, there's no need for me to hang around, explaining things. I'm going to go get me a little drink. I kind of need it."

His departure was scarcely noticed. Joss was staring at Mr. Duff. Mr. Duff was staring at Joss.

"Weatherby!" gasped Mr. Duff, at length. "What the devil are you doing here!"

There was a stern look on Joss's face.

"Don't go into side issues, J.B.," he said. "I demand an

explanation. Of the growth on the upper lip," he added. "It's frightful. Ghastly."

"Never mind——"

"There must be a certain code in these matters. Either a man is Grover Whalen or he is not Grover Whalen. If he is not, he has no right to wear a moustache like that."

"Never mind about my moustache. I asked you what you were doing here."

Joss raised his eyebrows.

"My dear J.B., when you madly dispensed with my services, you surely did not expect that a man of my gifts would be out of employment long? I was snapped up immediately. I have a sort of general commission to look after things here. You might call me the Claines Hall Führer."

"Steptoe said you were his valet."

"Yes, that's another way of putting it."

"There's something behind this."

"I see it's hopeless to try to conceal anything from one of your penetration. If you really want to know, J.B., I took on the job so that I could be with Miss Fairmile. You may possibly recall that I spoke of her with some warmth at our last meeting. Since then my feelings have, if such a thing were possible, deepened. If you would like it in words of one syllable, J.B., I'm in love."

"Oh?"

"A rather chilly comment on a great romance, but let it go. And now about the moustache. Explain fully, if you please."

Mr. Duff had begun to see that all things were working together for good.

"Listen," he said. "Do you want your job back?"

"I am prepared to hear what you have to say on the point."

"Then listen," said Mr. Duff.

Mr. Steptoe reappeared, looking refreshed.

"Told him?" he asked.

"I was just going to," said Mr. Duff. "Listen."

"Listen," said Mr. Steptoe.

"Now I've got it," said Joss. "You want me to listen. Why didn't you say so before?"

He stood in thoughtful silence, while Mr. Duff placed the facts in the case before him.

"Well?" said Mr. Steptoe.

"I beg your pardon? You spoke?"

"Will you?"

"Will I what? Oh, pinch the portrait? Of course, of course. I'm sorry I was distrait. I was just wondering how J.B. gets his food past that zareba. I suppose it works on a hinge, or something. Yes, of course, I shall be delighted."

"When? To-night?"

"To-night's the night," said Joss. "And now away with trivialities. Take these bones, Steptoe, and I'll show you how to roll them right."

11

NIGHT had fallen on Claines Hall, terminating a day which had been fraught with no little interest for many of those beneath its roof. But to only a limited number of these had it brought restful slumber. Lord Holbeton was awake. Chibnall was awake. Mr. Steptoe was awake. Joss was awake. Mrs. Chavender, also, had found it impossible to start getting her eight hours.

As a rule, this masterful woman shared with Napoleon the ability to sleep the moment the head touched the pillow. Others might count sheep, but she had no need for such adventitious aids to repose. She just creamed her face, basketed her Pekinese, climbed into bed, switched the light out and there she was.

Yet to-night she lay wakeful.

Ever since her return from Brighton, there had been noticeable in Mrs. Chavender's manner a strange moodiness. There was not a great deal of rollicking gaiety at Claines Hall, but from what there was she had held herself aloof. And if an observer could have seen her now, as she lay staring into the darkness, he would have remarked that this moodiness still prevailed.

It was as she heaved a weary sigh and fell to wondering whether to get up and go to the library for the book which she had been reading after dinner or to stay where she was and give the sandman another chance, that a faint whoofle from the direction of the door and a scratching of delicate paws on the woodwork told her that Patricia, her Peke, was up and about and wished to leave the room.

"Okay," said Mrs. Chavender, rather pleased that the problem had been settled for her. "Just a minute. Hold the line."

She turned on the light, and rose and donned a dressing-gown.

"Grass?" she said.

The Peke nodded briefly.

"I thought as much," said Mrs. Chavender. A slight disorder of the digestive tract, due to a surfeit of cheese, had been the cause of that visit to the vet, and on these occasions the dumb chum was apt to want to head for the lawn and nibble.

The French windows of the breakfast-room suggested themselves as the quickest way to the great outdoors. She proceeded thither and threw back the heavy curtains. The cool fragrance of the night, pouring in, seemed to bring momentary relief from the cares which were gnawing at her.

"There you are," she said. "Push along and help yourself. You'll find me in the library."

Patricia pottered out, and for some minutes roamed the dewy lawn, sniffing at this blade of grass and that like a connoisseur savouring rival vintages of brandy. Presently she found some excellent stuff, and became absorbed in it. Perhaps a quarter of an hour passed before she was at liberty to turn her attention elsewhere. When she did, she beheld a sight which brought her up with a sharp turn. She looked again, to make sure that she had not been mistaken. But her eyes had not deceived her. The light in the breakfast-room was on, and a man was standing in the window. He remained there for an instant, then drew the curtains.

Patricia stood staring. She was uncertain what to make of this. It might be all right, or it might not be all right. Time alone could tell. Off-hand, she was inclined to think it fishy.

Lord Holbeton, having drawn the curtains, took a knife from the pocket of his dressing-gown, and walked to the fireplace. There for a while he stood, exchanging glances with the portrait which hung above it.

It was in no mood of gay adventure that Lord Holbeton had embarked upon this midnight raid. He definitely did not like the job. Sally had urged him to it with girlish eagerness, but if it had been merely a question of obliging Sally, he would have been in bed. The motivating force behind his actions was the lust for gold.

Pondering over that disturbing encounter in the drive, he had suddenly realized that the moustached stranger must have been Mr. Duff, whom he knew to be established at the local inn, and he was able to understand now why Mr. Duff had shouted "Hey!" and come charging up at the double. Obviously, he had been anxious for a conference. It was the thought of how he had avoided that conference and an accurate estimate of what the effects of that avoidance on his always rather easily annoyed trustee would be that had spurred Lord Holbeton on to take action. Only by securing the portrait and delivering it at the earliest possible moment could he hope to wipe out the bad impression he must have made and bring the other to a frame of mind where he would reach for his fountain-pen and start writing cheques.

That was what had made him creep to the breakfast-room in the watches of the night. But it would not make him like it.

Oddly enough, the discovery that the window was open had not caused him any additional concern. The inference he drew was not that others beside himself were abroad in the darkness, but that whoever was supposed to lock up had been negligent. As a matter of fact, he had been intending to open it himself, for Sally, showing an easy familiarity with criminal procedure which he privately felt a really nice girl should not have possessed, had impressed it upon him that this must be made to look like an outside job.

He wrenched his gaze from that of the portrait, which he was beginning to find hypnotic, and opened his knife. If 'twere done, he felt, then 'twere well 'twere done quickly.

At this moment, the door flew open and there entered at a brisk pace a gentleman with a battle-axe. He advanced upon Lord Holbeton like a Danish warrior of the old school coming ashore from his galley, and the latter, dropping the knife, made an energetic attempt to get through the wall backwards. Not even on the occasion when he had called upon Mr. Duff and asked him for a thousand pounds so that he could go to Italy and have his voice trained had he been conscious of so urgent a desire to be elsewhere.

His disintegration was, however, only momentary, A second glance showed him that the martial figure was merely Chibnall.

Chibnall, like Mrs. Chavender, had found himself unable on retiring for the night to fall into a refreshing slumber. Airily, even mockingly, though he had received them at the time, Miss Pym's alarmist theories regarding Joss Weatherby had been sinking in throughout the day, and bedtime found him so entirely converted to them that sleep was out of the question.

Her remorseless reasoning had had its effect. Odd, he felt, that he had not spotted for himself that palpable flaw in the new valet's story, to which she had directed his attention. A young fellow, getting the bird from his father, gets it good and proper.

The father, just before administering the boot, does not say "Oh, by the way, you will be needing cash for expenses. Take these few hundreds." Where, then, as Miss Pym had asked, had Joss obtained the money in which he rolled?

And that stuff about Mayfair Men. That made you think a bit. Suave, presentable chaps they were, he had always been given to understand—just like this Weatherby.

At the moment when Lord Holbeton was entering the breakfast-room, Chibnall, too restless to remain between the sheets, had risen from his bed and gone to the window. And as Claines Hall was an L-shaped house and his room in the smaller part of the L, he had been admirably placed to see the light when it flashed on. It confirmed his worst fears. Two minutes later, he was on the spot, armed with the weapon which he had picked up while passing through the hall.

His disappointment at finding Lord Holbeton was great.

"Oh, it's you, m'lord?" he said dejectedly.

Lord Holbeton, though a crooner, was not without a certain sagacity. Some explanation of his presence would, he realized, be required, and he had thought one up.

"I say, Chibnall, I saw a light in here."

"So did I, m'lord."

"It was still on when I got here."

"Indeed, m'lord?"

"And I found the window open. Did you lock it no-night? You did? Well, it was open when I arrived. Odd."

"Very odd, m'lord."

"In fact, a bit rummy."

"Yes, m'lord."

At this moment, just when their conversation promised to develop along interesting lines, it seemed to both men that the end of the world had suddenly come. It was, as a matter of fact, only Patricia barking, but that was the impression they got.

If there was one thing this Pekinese prided herself on, it was her voice. She might not be big, she might look like a section of hearthrug, but she could bark. She was a coloratura soprano, who thought nothing of starting at A in alt and going steadily higher, and when she went off unexpectedly under their feet like a bomb, strong men were apt to lose their poise and skip like the high hills.

Until this moment, what had kept her silent was the fact that the man she had seen had been inside the house, looking out, and not outside the house, looking in. This had decided her to suspend judgment until she could investigate further. But as she made for the breakfast-room she had been feeling extremely dubious, and what had finally turned the scale was the sight of Lord Holbeton's dressing-gown. It was of a pattern so loud and vivid that it seemed absurd to suppose that it could encase an honest man. Patricia threw her head back, allowed her eyes to bulge to their extremest limit and went into a trill of accidental grace notes. And simultaneously Mrs. Chavender, in the library, and Mrs. Steptoe, in her bedroom, started up and hurried to the spot.

Mrs. Chavender, being nearer, got there first, and was just in time to see Patricia, a dog of action as well as words, bite Lord Holbeton shrewdly on the ankle.

The sight woke all the mother in her.

"What do you mean," she demanded sternly, snatching the Pekinese to her bosom, "by teasing the poor little thing when you know she's not well?"

It was while Lord Holbeton was endeavouring to select the most acid of the six replies which had suggested themselves to him that Mrs. Steptoe entered.

"What the heck?" enquired Mrs. Steptoe.

"Why, hullo, Mabel," said Mrs. Chavender. "You here? Doesn't anyone sleep in this joint?"

"I shouldn't think so," said Mrs. Steptoe tartly, "unless they're deaf."

"The dear old place has been a little on the noisy side to-night," admitted Mrs. Chavender. "Plenty of life and movement."

"I thought there had been a murder."

"I don't believe blood has actually been spilled, unless Lord Holbeton has lost a drop or two. From motives which she has not yet explained to me, though I assume they were sound, Patricia made a light supper off his leg."

"Chewed me to the bally bone," said Lord Holbeton morosely. "Get hydrophobia as likely as not."

Mrs. Steptoe addressed herself to the butler, appearing to consider him, in spite of the battle-axe, the most responsible party present.

"What is all this, Chibnall?"

"There was a light in the window, madam. I saw it from my

room, and felt it my duty to descend and investigate. On arrival, I found his lordship here. He, too, had observed the light. And he informs me that when he entered he found the window open."

"I opened it," said Mrs. Chavender, "to let Patricia out."

"Indeed, madam? I was not aware of that."

"She wanted to go out and eat grass."

"I quite understand, madam."

"Her tummy was upset."

"Precisely, madam. Grass in such circumstances is a recognized specific."

Whether Mrs. Steptoe was pleased or disappointed at this tame explanation of the affair, it would have been difficult to say. Her manner, when she spoke, was brusque, but then it always tended to be a little on that side.

"Well, if your dog is sure it has had all the grass it requires, Beatrice", she said, "perhaps we might all go back to bed and try to get a little sleep."

Mrs. Chavender intimated that that was just what she was thinking, and Lord Holbeton said he thought so, too, adding a little frostily that this would enable him to bathe his ankle in cold water and get in touch with the iodine bottle, thus possibly saving a human life.

"Shut that window, Chibnall."

"Very good, madam."

"Well, good night, all," said Mrs. Chavender. "No, Patricia, no second helping."

She passed from the room, followed by Lord Holbeton, limping reproachfully. Patricia gave a final shrill comment on the dressing-gown before signing off.

Mrs. Steptoe clicked her tongue impatiently. Chibnall was standing at the window, peering out as if rapt by the beauty of the night, and she disapproved. When she told butlers to close windows, she expected an imitation of forked lightning.

"Chibnall!"

"Madam?"

"Be quick."

"Excuse me, madam."

"Well, what is it?"

The butler had closed the window and withdrawn into the room. There was an urgency in his manner.

"I fancied I saw dim figures stealing across the lawn, madam."

"What?"

"Yes, madam. Two dim figures. They appeared to be coming in this direction."

"What on earth," asked Mrs. Steptoe, not unreasonably, "would dim figures be doing on the lawn at this time of night?"

"Burglars, no doubt, madam. If I might——"

He moved to the switch, and the next moment the room was in darkness, a fact that seemed to make an unfavourable impression on Mrs. Steptoe.

"You poor fish," she cried, forgetting in her agitation the respect due to butlers, "what on earth are you doing?"

"I thought it advisable to extinguish the light, madam, in order not to alarm these persons."

To a sentimentalist it would have seemed a kindly, rather pretty thought, but the exclamation that proceeded from the darkness suggested that Mrs. Steptoe found such consideration for the nervous systems of the criminal classes hypersensitive.

"I am in favour, if it can be contrived, madam, of catching the miscreants red-handed. I have closed the window. If they break the glass, that will be proof of their unlawful intentions. As they enter the room, I will switch the light on and confront them."

"Oh! I see. Well, don't let go of that battle-axe."

"I have it in readiness, madam. If I might make the suggestion, it would be best if we now preserved a complete silence."

They did so. There was a long moment of suspense. Then something tinkled in the darkness. Glass had fallen to the floor.

The light flashed out. It shone on Mr. Steptoe, blinking, and behind him Joss, whose air was one of courteous interest.

If Joss had been aware that the idea of lending to the night's proceedings the aspect of an outside job had occurred independently to Sally, he would have taken it as additional proof, if such were needed, that she and he were twin souls, for it was what he had thought of himself. Mr. Steptoe, a blunt, direct man, had been unable to see the point of getting out of the house merely in order to get into it again, but Joss had overruled him. These things, he had explained, should be done properly or not at all.

"Well!" said Mrs. Steptoe.

"Oh, there you are," said Joss heartily.

"Weatherby!"

"Madam? Ah, good evening, Chibnall," said Joss, not wishing to leave him out of the conversation.

"What the heck do you think you're doing? And you, Howard," demanded Mrs. Steptoe, turning on her mate, "what do you think *you're* doing?"

It was a question which Mr. Steptoe could see was prompted by a genuine desire for information, and he was in a position to answer it. But he shrank from doing so. He seemed to swallow something which his thorax was not quite wide enough to accommodate with comfort, and cast at Joss the look of a drowning man anxious to be thrown a life-line.

Joss did not fail him.

"I am afraid, madam," he said smoothly, "that I am wholly to blame for this untimely intrusion. Lying awake in bed just now, I happened to hear the nightingale, and feeling that Mr. Steptoe ought not to miss this treat I woke him and suggested that he should accompany me into the garden."

"Oh?"

"Yes, madam. We could not see what flowers were at our feet, nor what soft incense hung upon the boughs, but we managed to catch a glimpse of the bird, did we not, sir?"

"Yeah," said Mr. Steptoe. "It was a whopper."

"Quite well-developed," assented Joss. "And vocally in tremendous form. We listened entranced. 'Thou wast not made for death, immortal bird,' said Mr. Steptoe, and I agreed with him. I often say that there is no melody quite like the song of the nightingale. Mr. Steptoe feels the same."

"Yeah," said Mr. Steptoe.

"He put forward the rather interesting theory that this was quite possibly the selfsame song that found a path through the sad heart of Ruth when, sick for home, she stood in tears amid the alien corn. I thought there might be something in it."

"Weatherby," said Mrs. Steptoe, "have you been drinking?"

"Only of the Pierian fount, madam."

The intellectual pressure of the conversation was becoming too much for Mrs. Steptoe.

"All this," she said, "doesn't explain why you come busting in through windows."

"In his anxiety to reach the garden, madam, Mr. Steptoe unfortunately omitted to take his latchkey with him, and we found ourselves shut out. Not wishing to disturb the house, I suggested that we should make an unobtrusive entrance through a window."

"Oh?" said Mrs. Steptoe. She stood a while in thought, then jerked an impervious hand towards the door. "Howard, go to bed."

"Yes, honey," said Mr. Steptoe obediently, and shambled out. His mind was in a whirl, but there emerged from the welter one coherent thought. Like the poet Keats on a similar occasion, he wanted a drink. Oh, he was saying to himself as he mounted the stairs, for a beaker full of the warm South, full of the true, the blushful Hippocrene, and by a singular piece of good fortune he had the makings in a flask on the table beside his bed. His rather careworn manner softened, and he sucked in his lips in pleasant anticipation.

"Shut that window," said Mrs. Steptoe.

"Very good, madam," said Joss.

"Though it's hardly worth while after you've been punching holes in it," said Mrs. Steptoe, and left the room stiffly.

She was surprised to discover, as she reached the foot of the stairs, that she had been accompanied by her butler, and paused to ascertain the reason for this mateyness on his part.

"Yes, Chibnall?"

"I wonder if I might speak to you for a moment, madam?"

"You've picked a swell time for chatting. I need my beauty sleep. Well, all right, make it snappy."

"It is with reference to the young man Weatherby, madam".

"What about him?"

"I am not easy in my mind about his bona fides, madam. I find his behaviour suspicious. Were you aware, madam, that he arrived at the Hall in his personal automobile?"

"Did he?"

"Yes, madam. That was my reason for showing him to the drawing-room. I naturally supposed him to be a guest."

Mrs. Steptoe pursed her lips. In her native California, of course, the incident would have been without significance. It is a very impoverished valet in the Golden State who does not dash up to the door in his private car. But in England, she knew, different conditions prevailed.

"Odd," she said.

"Yes, madam. It is also unusual for a young fellow in his position to give the butler in the establishment where he is taking service a present of ten pounds."

"Did he do that?"

"Yes, madam."

"H'm."

"A suggestion which has been advanced by a friend of mine to whom I confided the circumstances is that he is one of these Mayfair Men who, having recently pulled off a big job, is using the Hall for what is termed a hide-out."

"Nonsense."

"Just as you say, madam. But he seems a very peculiar valet to me. I certainly think it would be advisable to notify the police, and have them institute enquiries into his antecedents."

"No, that's out," said Mrs. Steptoe, decidedly. Chibnall had agitated her, but even in her agitation she did not lose sight of the fact that Joss, if a peculiar—and possibly a criminal—valet, was an extremely efficient one. By what magic he had wrought the miracle, she could not say, but he had sent the hick Howard down to dinner on the previous night looking not merely respectable but refulgent. His shirt had shone like a lighthouse, so that Baronets gaped at the sight of it. So had his shoes. And as for his collar and tie, they could have been used as exhibits in a lecture on what the smart dresser should wear. It would be madness to put the police on the trail of this wonder-man.

On the other hand, she did not want to wake up one morning and find the place looted.

"I'm not going to have the house littered up with cops. You had better watch him."

"Very good, madam. I was about to suggest that, if the idea meets with your approval, I should pass the remainder of the night in the breakfast-room. This would enable me to guard the tapestries."

"He can't be after those."

"They are extremely valuable."

"Yes, but if he had been trying to swipe them, would he have taken Mr. Steptoe with him?"

"There is that, of course, madam."

"Still, I'm all for your spending the night in the breakfast-room. I don't like leaving that broken window. Snap into it."

"Very good, madam."

In the breakfast-room, meanwhile, Joss, having closed the window, had been standing in a train of thought. What had started this train of thought had been the sight of the knife which Lord Holbeton had dropped on the floor. He was at a loss to account for its presence there, but it seemed to him to come under the head of manna from heaven. Two things are essential to the purloining of a portrait from a country house—the first, opportunity; the second, some implement for removing the thing from its frame. He now had both.

He picked up the knife and, like Lord Holbeton, crossed to the fireplace. There, also like Lord Holbeton, he stood gazing at the portrait, thinking—though this Lord Holbeton had not done—what a remarkably good bit of work it was. Then, bringing up a chair and standing on it, he was about to start carving, when a voice, speaking in his rear, brought him to the ground as if he had been lassoed.

"Ah!" said the voice.

Mrs. Chavender was standing in the doorway.

12

Mrs. CHAVENDER'S appearance was always striking. It was now rendered additionally so by the circumstances that she, like himself, was armed to the teeth. There was a large knife in her hand. It made her look like Lady Macbeth.

Too well bred to comment on this, Joss opened the conversation with a civil "Good evening."

"We meet again, Mrs. Chavender."

"We do, young Weatherby."

"You are doubtless surprised——"

"No, I'm not. Sally Fairmile told me you were here. And I know—— Sh!" said Mrs. Chavender, breaking off her remarks. "There's someone coming."

"There always is in this house. It's the Claines Hall Curse."

"Meet me in the library."

"Where is it?"

"Along the passage. I want to talk with you, young man. Yes, Chibnall?"

The butler was entering, bowed down beneath the weight of blankets and pillows. Though all enthusiasm to begin this vigil of his, he had taken time out to go to his room and collect the materials for making himself as comfortable as possible.

"Mrs. Steptoe desired me to pass the remainder of the night in here, madam."

"Why on earth?"

"One of the windows has become broken, madam, and Mrs Steptoe is uneasy about having it left. It is possible," said Chibnall darkly, "that there may be suspicious characters about."

"Oh? Well, sooner you than me. Good night."

"Good night, madam."

Mrs. Chavender sailed from the room, and Chibnall looked at Joss coldly.

"Still here?"

"Just going. Tell me, my dear Chibnall, would you describe

90

this as one of Claines Hall's ordinary nights? I merely want to know what to expect."

"Took you quite a time to close that window."

"No, no. I did it like a flash. But I was then engaged in conversation by the lady who has just left us. Are you really going to sleep in here?"

"I am."

"I'll bet you're not. You won't get a wink. I've tried dossing in chairs myself. No, what you ought to do, my dear fellow," said Joss winningly, "is to toddle back to your little bed and curl up your pink toes. Nobody will know."

"Thank you. I prefer to do my duty."

"Oh? Well, in that case, good night."

"Good night."

As Joss made his way to the library, he was finding the atmosphere too heavily charged with mystery for comfort. Chibnall had been mysterious. So had Mrs. Chavender. Mrs. Chavender's mysteriousness would no doubt shortly be explained, but there seemed no hope of penetrating the inscrutability of the butler. At the Rose and Crown that morning, and right through the day, Chibnall had been all that was cordial and friendly, and now he was a changed man, curt in his speech and showing a tendency to shoot sharp, sidelong glances. Joss found it puzzling.

The enigmatic attitude of Chibnall, however, could wait. The immediate subject on the agenda paper was the enigmatic attitude of Mrs. Chavender. It was with a lively desire for enlightenment that he entered the library.

"Oh, there you are," said Mrs. Chavender. "Shut the door."

Joss shut the door.

"Sit down."

Joss sat down.

"Now, where were we?" said Mrs. Chavender.

Joss was able to refresh her memory.

"You had begun by saying that you were not surprised to find me on the premises because Miss Fairmile had told you I was here. Is her name really Sally? Capital, capital. A delightful name. One of my favourites. It's positively amazing," said Joss, warming to his subject, "how everything seems to be working out, as if I had had it done to my specifications. She's beautiful. She has a lovely voice. And her name's Sally. Not a flaw in the set-up, as far as I can see."

Mrs. Chavender seemed perplexed.

"Would you mind telling me what, if anything, you're talking about?"

"I should have mentioned," Joss explained, "that I love this young Fairmile. It hit me like the kick of a mule the instant I saw her. Romeo had the same experience. And Chibnall."

"Oh? Well, we can go into that later."

"Any time that suits you," said Joss courteously. "Well, after saying that you were not surprised to find me here, you added the words: 'And I know . . .' At that point you heard Chibnall coming, and switched off. You never did get around to telling me what it was that you knew."

"Well, I'll tell you now. I know why you're here. Jimmy Duff sent you to swipe that portrait."

"What an extraordinary idea."

"Is it? Well, let me tell you I've had the whole story from an authoritative source. Mrs. Steptoe told me that Jimmy had made an offer for the thing and she had turned him down. And the next thing that happens is that you sneak into the place."

"Not sneak. I bowled up to the front door in my car."

"You being Jimmy's—what did you say you were?"

"Best friend and severest critic?"

"That was it. Well, it's all pretty plain, isn't it? Can you beat it?" said Mrs. Chavender, her voice softening. "After fifteen years Jimmy's still that way about me. I'm darned if I'd have thought he had that much sentiment in him. It looks as if I'd been getting him wrong all this time. When you told me he was still a bachelor, I supposed he had stayed one because he liked it. And all the time it was because he was so crazy about me that he couldn't look at anybody else. And the way he figures it out is that, even if he has lost me, he can still have my portrait, to remember me by. If you don't think that's sweet and lovely and touching and wonderful, maybe you'll tell me what is."

It was not for Joss to destroy this gossamer fabric of romance with the acid-cleaning fluid of truth. He nodded sympathetically.

"Yes, he's a rare soul. He reminds me a little of Sir Galahad. But he didn't send me down here. At the moment when I signed on at Claines Hall, there existed between J.B. and myself a slight coolness. He had fired me."

"What did you do to him?"

"Not a thing, except sling him out of his office."

"I don't get this. You aren't going to tell me that when I came into that room just now you weren't starting to cut the portrait out of its frame."

"Quite true. I was."

"Well, then."

"But J.B. had got in touch with me since my arrival here. This affair is a lot more complicated than you think it. All sorts of dark currents are running beneath the quiet surface of life at Claines Hall. May I speak confidentially?"

"Shoot."

"This will go no further?"

"Not through me."

"Well, then, I am acting not only for J.B., but for Mr. Steptoe."

"Howard Steptoe?"

"Yes. It was he who brought J.B. and me together. He needs the stuff, and it was his original intention to put the deal through by himself. Finding, however, that he required moral support, he called me in."

"Well, listen," said Mrs. Chavender vehemently. "I'm in on this, too. I don't mind giving Howard Steptoe his cut, but when Jimmy starts paying out, five hundred pounds has got to be earmarked for me. You say Howard Steptoe needs the stuff. Well, take a look at someone else who does."

Joss was astounded.

"You?"

"Me."

"But I thought you were a millionairess."

"So I was till about a year ago. Remember the Battersby crash?"

"Were you in that?"

"Up to the eyebrows. I lost my chemise. When the accountants had finished raking over the ashes, I found I'd just about enough left to pay Patricia's licence and a modest annual dress bill."

"Well, well, well!" said Joss. "Well, well, well, well, well!"

There was a silence. Mrs. Chavender was wrestling with an obviously powerful emotion.

"Got a cigarette?" she said.

"I'm afraid not."

"Then I'll have to have one of my own. And I hate them. I was hoping you might have something better."

Joss was adjusting his faculties to this sensational revelation.

"You've kept it pretty dark. The servants' hall knows nothing of this. Mrs. Barlow was saying to me only this evening that you were a female creosote."

Mrs. Chavender puffed at her cigarette in silence for a moment. Then she showed that she was her old self again by emitting a deep chuckle.

"You bet I kept it dark. And I'll tell you why. You've met Mabel?"

"You mean Sally?"

"I don't mean Sally. I mean Mabel. Mabel Steptoe."

"Oh, Mrs. Steptoe? Yes, of course. A delightful woman. She held me spellbound with her views on Corot."

"Did she mention her views on poor relations?"

"No, we didn't get around to those."

"Well, keep your eye on young Sally Fairmile, and you'll soon know what they are. She believes in treating them rough. Talk about oppressed minorities."

The library swam before Joss.

"You mean she bullies that sweet girl?"

"Well, she doesn't beat her and she doesn't starve her, but that's about all you can say. No, that's not fair. She's quite kind to her really, I suppose. Put it this way. Young Sally's position in the home is about that of an unpaid lady's maid."

"Monstrous!"

"What mine would be, if it ever came out that I was broke, I don't know. A sort of female butler without portfolio, I guess. Mabel has her points—I'm very fond of her—but she's one of those women who can't help taking it out of the under-dog. You daren't let her get on top of you. You've got to keep her under your thumb. That's what I've been doing this last year, since I came to live with her. Thank God for giving me a curling lip and a commanding eye. Not that they would be any good, if she didn't think I had a weak heart and all the money in the world and was going to hand in my dinner-pail at any moment and leave my millions to her."

"The woman is a ghoul."

"No, she's not. She's all right, provided you're in a position

to sit on her head. And so far I have been. But, oh baby, if I
can't raise that five hundred pounds!"

This second mention of that specific sum interested Joss.

"Why do you want that exact amount?"

"It's a debt I've got to pay. One of these debts of honour.
And if I can't get the money any other way, I shall have to ask
Mabel for it, and then the whole facts about my financial position
will come out and I shall sink to the level of a fifth-rate
power. Say, have you ever presented the prizes at a girls'
school?"

Joss said that he had never had that experience.

"Well, don't," said Mrs. Chavender, and relapsed into a
pensive silence. She seemed to be re-living a scene which, if the
frown on her fine forehead was to be taken as evidence, had not
been an agreeable one. Her eyes, as she drew at her cigarette,
were clouded.

"Don't you do it," she said, at length. "There's something
about the atmosphere that does something to you. There they
are, and you think of the time when you were that age, with
the world before you, and it's as if you had gone on a bender and
got full to the gills of vintage champagne. I presented the prizes
at a girls' school yesterday."

"Yes, I remember you telling me that you were going to. You
wanted something to say to the inmates, and I suggested 'Hullo,
girls,' which you seemed to feel would be inadequate. Did you
think of something better on the way down?"

"Did I! I made the speech of a lifetime. I had them tearing
up the seats and rolling in the aisles."

"Good," said Joss.

"Not so good," said Mrs. Chavender. "Because I hadn't the
sense to stop there and take a bow and get off. I had to go and
overdo it. Shall I tell you what happened?"

"I'm all agog."

"Well, I must begin by mentioning that the Warden of this
seashore Sing-Sing, in her few words of introduction, had spoken
of a new gymnasium, or some dam' thing, which they were
planning to build, and had hoped that all parents would contribute generously to this very deserving cause, as the school
expected to be punched in the pocket-book for at least two
thousand of the best and brightest. She then said that Mrs.
Chavender would now address you on Ideals and the Future Life,

and I spat out my lozenge and advanced to the footlights. And, as I say, I wowed them. And then, when the applause had died down and I could hear myself speak, I heard myself speak. And do you know what I was saying? I was saying that I would give five hundred pounds towards their blasted gymnasium, if three others would do the same."

"Ah!" said Joss.

"You may well say 'Ah!' Mark you, even though my eloquence had reduced me to a condition where I could have walked straight into any Inebriates' Home and no questions asked, I thought I was playing it pretty safe. I remembered the gloomy silence which had greeted that gag about contributing generously, and while the room re-echoed to the salvos of applause and the dust went up from the stamping of six hundred girlish feet, I kept saying to myself: 'All may yet be well, old sport. I think so. I hope so.' And would you believe it, a couple a minutes later two nitwits with criminal faces had sprung forward with tears in their eyes, shouting that they were with me. And a moment later another certifiable idiot had said the same. So there I was. The best I could do, which wasn't much, was to say I had left my cheque-book at home, but that they would hear from me in due course. So now, young Weatherby, you know why I want five hundred pounds."

Her admirably clear exposition of the facts had left Joss in no doubt on that point.

"You must certainly have it," he said. "As I see it, we form a syndicate. About how much do you think J.B. would go to?"

"Apparently Mabel didn't let him get as far as talking figures. But I think a thousand pounds would be cheap in the circumstances, don't you?"

"Dirt cheap. An absolutely authentic Weatherby—his Palm Beach period—should fetch that, and more."

"Would five hundred be enough for you and Howard Steptoe to split?"

"Don't worry about me. I don't come in on the money end of it. What I want is my job back, or possibly I may stand out for being made head of the Art Department. I shall have to think it over."

"I'd stand out."

"Yes, perhaps I will. I'm not thinking of myself. It would be such a grand thing for the firm to have a head of the Art Department like me."

"Then what's the procedure?" Do I run up to London and see Jimmy?"

"He's at the inn at Loose Chippings."

"That's convenient. I'll look in there."

"And now to form a plan of campaign. How do we act for the best? It's not going to be easy. Did you notice anything about Chibnall just now?"

"His pyjamas?"

"No, though I agree that they were striking. Somehow one always pictures a butler in a nightshirt. I was referring to his manner. I didn't like it. He's stopped calling me 'Sir.' Also, his eye was cold."

"You think he suspects?"

"I'm convinced of it."

"You can outsmart him. Just choose a time when he isn't prowling. And I'll tell you when that'll be. During the garden party."

"Of course. I suppose a butler has to buttle like nobody's business during a garden party."

"He won't have a free minute. And there's another thing. All the nobility and gentry for miles around will be at the garden party. The place will become practically a thieves' kitchen. This will distribute suspicion."

"You think of everything."

From somewhere in the distance there sounded a shrill, impatient bark. Mrs. Chavender rose hurriedly.

"I must go. That's Patricia what-the-helling. She doesn't like being left alone."

"Your bloodhound?"

"My Peke, God bless her."

"Is that the one Miss Fairmile brushes?"

"It's one of the ones she brushes. She's an admirable dog-brusher. Tactful and soothing. All right, my angel rabbit, Mother's coming. By the way," said Mrs. Chavender, pausing at the door, "did I understand you to say you loved Sally?"

"That's right."

"Well, I don't know how it's going to affect your plans, but she told me this morning, when we were driving to Lewes, that she was engaged to this Lord Holbeton you may have seen pottering about the place. All right, all right, all right," said Mrs. Chavender, as the imperious summons sounded once more from above, "I'm coming, I tell you. The way these darned Pekes keep you on the jump, you'd think they thought you went around in spiked shoes and running shorts."

⋆ 13 ⋆

IT was not until late on the following morning that Sally learned from Lord Holbeton of the stirring doings which had enlivened the watches of the previous night. She had breakfasted early and he, nature having taken its toll of the tired frame, had breakfasted late. He found her eventually in the stable yard, preparing to set out for London in the two-seater, and proceeded to pour forth his tale, omitting no detail, however slight. In particular, he stressed more than was perhaps actually essential what might be termed the Pekinese *motif*. Women love men for the dangers they have passed, but Sally could not help feeling that there was no need for him to show her the sore place on his leg three times.

Having already observed that the portrait of Mrs. Chavender was still in its frame, she had of course been prepared for a record of failure, and she was fair-minded enough, now that the circumstances had been placed before her, to recognize that the failure had been an honourable one. A man can but do his best, and in enterprises of the type which her betrothed had undertaken privacy is the first essential. She quite realized that he could not have been expected to operate successfully with butlers popping in all the time.

Nevertheless, though she tried to fight against it, she could not check a certain sense of disappointment. Perhaps it was that other story which he had told her yesterday, of his race for life in the drive, that coloured her view. At any rate, she was left with the feeling, coming to her now for the first time and giving her an uncomfortable shock as if scales had fallen from her eyes, that Lord Holbeton, though *svelte* and willowy and unquestionably good at singing *Trees*, was not quite the man she had thought him. "Feet of clay" was the distasteful phrase that forced itself on the mind.

Having sympathized with her loved one's sore leg and declined, though cordially invited to do so, to look at it for the fourth time, she applied herself to the problem of what was to be done next.

99

Her immediate impulse was to seek out Mr. Duff and make a report. After that unfortunate affair in the drive, she felt, he must be needing reassurance that his interests were being looked after. But her time was not her own. Mrs. Steptoe having suddenly decided that in the matter of extra help for the garden party it would be madness to trust to local talent, she was being dispatched to London to engage metropolitan waiters, hard-bitten and experienced veterans who could be relied on.

The quest for these occupied the whole of the early afternoon, and the hands of the church clock were pointing to half-past four as she entered Loose Chippings on her homeward journey. And she was just speculating on the chances of Mr. Duff being at the Rose and Crown at this hour, when she saw him in the High Street. He was standing in a sort of trance, staring at the statue of the late Anthony Briggs.

To those who find themselves marooned in Loose Chippings, about the only thing offered in the way of mental stimulus is the privilege of looking at the statue erected by a few friends and admirers to the memory of the late Anthony Briggs, J.P., for many years Parliamentary representative for the local division. You can walk up the High Street and look at it from the front, or you can walk down the High Street and look at it from the back. (By standing in the middle of the High Street you can also look at it sideways, but this is a technicality which need not detain us.)

Mr. Duff at the moment was looking at it from the front, but without any sensation of uplift. Even if you are interested in statues of members of Parliament, their fascination tends to relax its grip after you have seen them forty or fifty times. For Mr. Duff, the late Anthony Briggs had definitely lost his magic. He was also feeling that he had seen all that he wanted to of Loose Chippings.

And he was just thinking what a real pleasure it would be to touch off a stick of dynamite under the late Anthony Briggs and—more generally—that it would be all right with him if the entire town of Loose Chippings were to be submerged in molten lava like the Cities of the Plain, when he heard his name called by a feminine voice, and the hideous thought that it was Mrs. Chavender who had spoken brought him out of his meditations, quivering in every limb.

"Oh, it's you!" he said, relieved.

"Can I talk to you, Mr. Duff?" said Sally.

"Sure," said Mr. Duff. He did not like talking to girls, but it was something to do.

"Will you give me some tea?"

"If you like."

"There's a place just along here. The Gardenia."

Mr. Duff was familiar with it, or at least with its exterior. The Gardenia Tea Shoppe stood almost immediately opposite the Rose and Crown, and many a time had he shied like a startled horse at the sight of the tiers of disgusting, bilious-looking pastry displayed in its window. Left to himself, he would have avoided an establishment the mere appearance of which made him feel that his indigestion was coming on again, but he supposed that if his companion wanted to go there, he must humour her. He climbed into the car, and they drove off.

Like all Tea Shoppes in English country towns, the Gardenia was hermetically sealed. No crevice in its walls allowed fresh air to steal in and dilute its peculiar atmosphere. A warm, sickly scent of buns and cake and hot bread and chocolate seemed to Mr. Duff to twine itself about him as he entered, and he closed his eyes with a faint shudder. Coming back to this world after an interval of semi-consciousness, he found that the ladylike waitress had set their repast before them.

"I ordered buns," said Sally, who had the healthy appetite of youth. "Do you like buns?"

"I do not like buns," said Mr. Duff.

"I'm sorry. Some fancy cakes, please."

"Fancy cakes, right," said the ladylike waitress.

"Couldn't touch 'em," moaned Mr. Duff.

"Oh, but you must," urged Sally, "now they're here. I can't eat alone. Just one."

"Well, one," said Mr. Duff weakly. "You like to hear what this is going to do to me? Just going to kill me, that's all."

He picked feebly at the gruesome lump of cream and pastry which had been placed before him: then, catching the waitress's eye, attacked it with more animation. She was a tall, severe young woman with pince-nez, and there was something about her that reminded him of a strong-willed nurse of childhood days who had always made him eat his fat.

They sat for some moments in silence. Sally, though consumed with curiosity about the moustache, forbore to make any reference to it. Deciding that it was one of those painful disfigurements to which one cannot allude, she finished her tea and came to business.

"Well," she said brightly, for she had determined to be bright, "I suppose you are wondering what has been happening?"

Mr. Duff, before replying, sent a questing tongue in search of a piece of the fancy cake which had adhered to the outskirts of the foliage. He secured it at length, but the struggle had been a hard one and had deepened the moroseness of his mood.

"I know what's been happening," he said, with a snort. "That young loafer you say you want to marry has been running like a rabbit every time I get near him."

"Yes, he told me about that. But, you see——"

"I've said it before, and I'll say it again. If George Holbeton had two ounces more brain, just two ounces more, he would be half-witted. The poor wet smack!"

Not for the first time, Sally found this man's conversation an irritant.

"Don't call him a poor wet smack!"

"If you only knew what I'd like to call him."

"Of course he ran away. Who wouldn't, with people bounding out at him on every side with false moustaches on? He thought you were a homicidal maniac. George is very high-strung."

"You couldn't string him too high for me."

Sally was silent for a space. Prudence had whispered to her that it were wiser not to say what she would have liked to say. Whatever his spiritual defects, J. B. Duff was the man who signed the cheques, and must at all costs be conciliated. She wrestled with her better self, and finally succeeded in bringing it to the surface by the scruff of its neck.

"Well, anyway," she said, with the strained sweetness of a girl of spirit who is keeping that spirit under with an effort almost too great for her frail strength, "he hasn't just been sitting around, doing nothing. He's full of zeal. He had a try for the portrait last night."

"And didn't get it, I'll bet."

"It wasn't his fault. The butler came in with a battle-axe. He is going to try again."

"He needn't. You can tell him it's off. I've made other arrangements."

"What do you mean?"

"What I say. I've put the matter in other hands."

"Whose?"

"Never mind."

Sally gave a little jump.

"Not Mr. Weatherby's?"

"Yes! He's attending to the whole thing."

Sally sat biting her lip. Her face was grave. This, she could not but feel, was serious. Brief though her acquaintance with Joss had been, she had seen enough of him to be aware that he would be a formidable rival.

"Now there," proceeded Mr. Duff, "is a young fellow that amounts to something. I don't say he isn't as fresh as an April breeze. He is. I don't say I haven't often wanted to hit him with a brick. I have. But I do say he's got get-up in him. Enterprise. Resource. Look," said Mr. Duff in a sort of ecstasy, "at the way he bounced me out of my office that time, just because he didn't want me giving him hell in front of you. Quick as a flash. Why you don't marry him, instead of fooling around with your string bean of a Holbeton, beats me."

Sally smiled a wintry smile.

"He hasn't asked me."

"He will."

"And, if he did, I should remind him that we are practically strangers."

"He says he's crazy about you."

"And, if that wasn't enough, I should add that I love George."

"Now, why?" mused Mr. Duff, mystified. "I can't understand how you get that idea. I wonder if in the whole of England there is a fatter-headed chump than George Holbeton. Maybe. Somewhere. Take a bit of finding, though."

It is not often that a girl has occasion to grind her teeth, but Sally did so now. With a stupendous effort she once more forced herself to remain courteous. Her better self had made a dive for freedom, but she grabbed it just in time and dragged it back kicking and struggling.

"But, Mr. Duff, you must be fair. If George gets the por-trait——"

"He won't."

"Well, suppose I do?"

"You?"

"Yes. If I do, will you keep your promise and give George his money?"

Her words had opened up new vistas to Mr. Duff. He saw no objection whatever to a little competition. A corps of assistants is better than a single assistant. Quite possibly, he reflected, this enterprise might be one of those things which require the woman's touch.

"Sure," he said. "A bargain's a bargain."

"Then you can expect it to-morrow."

"As soon as that?"

"To-morrow evening, at about this time."

"You seem pretty certain of yourself."

"I am."

"Don't forget young Weatherby will be working against you."

"I don't care who's working against me. And now I must be going. Mrs. Steptoe is giving a big garden party to-morrow, and she will be wanting me."

It was in a somewhat more optimistic mood that Mr. Duff left the Gardenia Tea Shoppe and crossed the street to the Rose and Crown. In the lounge he found Joss waiting for him. To Joss, as well as to Sally, it had occurred that his principal ought to be informed at an early date of the night's doings. Mr. Duff, as he saw it, was rather in the position of a master-mind of the criminal world directing a gang of pock-marked Mexicans, and such persons like to keep in touch.

"Oh, it's you?" said Mr. Duff, regarding his young friend without enthusiasm. The fancy cake had begun to put in its deadly work, and that brief spurt of happiness had already died away, leaving behind it a leaden despondency.

This despondency was not lessened by the fact that his companion was looking as disgustingly fit and cheerful as ever. In spite of last night's bit of bad news, there was nothing of the heart-broken lover about Joss. He was, as has been indicated before, a resilient young man, and though Mrs. Chavender's sensational revelation had given him an unpleasant jolt at the moment, he had quickly recovered from the blow. He had seen Lord Holbeton here and there about the place since his arrival at Claines Hall, and he declined to believe that a girl like Sally could really love a man like that. Just one of those absurd mis-understandings, he felt, over which they would have a good laugh later.

"Come to give you the latest news, J.B.," he said. "I thought you would like to have it. Let's step into the bar parlour. It's quieter there, and you look as if you could do with a quick shot."

It being Miss Pym's afternoon off, the bar parlour was being presided over by a pot-boy; and though this robbed it of much of its social glitter, Joss was not sorry that the future Mrs. Chibnall was absent. There are moments when one likes to sit exchanging light nothings with charming women, others when the business note must be stressed. He ordered a small draught ale for himself, and for his companion, whom he saw to be in need of something more authoritative, a double brandy and split-soda. This done, he delivered his report.

"In a word," he concluded. "Fortune did not smile. But you will be glad to learn that I propose to make another attempt to-morrow. News may have reached you of a garden party that will break out at the Hall in the afternoon. That will be my hour, J.B. Not a soul around. Everybody out on the lawn, swilling tea and sucking down strawberries. I shall be able to saunter in and help myself at my leisure."

Mr. Duff seemed to think well of the idea. It occurred to him that Sally, speaking so confidently of delivering the portrait on the morrow, must also have had in her mind the strategic possibilities offered by a garden party.

"I suppose that's what that girl was planning," he said. "She seemed pretty sure of delivering the goods."

"What girl?"

"The one you're stuck on. I've forgotten her name. Little shrimp with blue eyes."

Joss raised his eyebrows.

"Are you by any chance alluding to Miss Fairmile?"

"That's right. Fairmile. That's the name."

"Then, for your information, she is not a little shrimp."

"She is, too."

"She is not. I've seen shrimps, and I've seen Miss Fairmile, and there is no resemblance whatever. If what you are trying to say in your uncouth way is that she is as tiny and graceful as a Tanagra figurine, then I am with you. But this loose talk about shrimps must cease, and cease immediately. What do you mean about saying she would deliver the goods?"

"I met her just now. She yoo-hooed at me from her car, and

we got talking. She's engaged to a fellow I'm trustee for. Young chap named Holbeton."

"So I hear. Dam' silly idea, isn't it? Of course, she'll have to break it off. We can't have that sort of thing going on."

"And she said that if I would give him his money, so that they could get married, she would swipe that portrait for me."

"To which you very properly replied that the matter was in the hands of your accredited agent?"

"No, I didn't. I told her to go right ahead."

Joss was shocked.

"You mean you encouraged her in this mad scheme? You wern't appalled at the thought of that lovely girl marrying a bird who looks as if he were trying to swallow a tennis ball?"

"Matter of fact, I told her she was a fool to have anything to do with him. I said she ought to marry you."

"You did? Then I'm sorry I called you a louse."

"You didn't."

"Well, I was just going to. So you advised her to marry me, eh?" said Joss, laying an affectionate hand on his companion's knee. "You advised her to marry me, did you, old pal?"

"Sooner than him," said Mr. Duff, moving the knee. "Personally, if I was a girl, I'd rather be dead in a ditch than marry either of you."

"Another double brandy for this gentleman," said Joss to the pot-boy. "And slip a shot of some little-known Asiatic poison in it. You're a hard nut, J.B. I suppose there *is* a heart of gold beneath that rugged exterior of yours, but I should require more than a verbal assurance on the point."

Mr. Duff regarded his glass dubiously.

"I don't know if I ought to have another. If I'm not in for one of my dyspeptic attacks, the signs have got me fooled. It's the cooking in this joint. Passes belief. You'd think they'd have learned to fry an egg by now. Well, all right, since it's here."

He sat sipping it after Joss had left him, and his dubiousness increased. Too late, he remembered that his medical adviser had warned him against spirits. By the time Joss was nearing the Hall (walking pensively, for Mr. Duff's words had given him food for thought), he had come definitely to the conclusion that he had better go to his room and lie down a while.

And he had just pushed open the main door of the Rose and Crown with that end in view, when there came to his ears, speak-

ing from within, a feminine voice. It was fifteen years since he
had heard it, but he had not forgotten those rich contralto notes.

"Well, when he comes back," it was saying, "tell him that
Mrs. Chavender called and wants to see him right away."

For one agelong instant, Mr. Duff stood frozen in his tracks.
Then life returned to the rigid limbs, and he darted back into
the High Street, looking about him in a panic for a place of refuge.

It was only too evident that this old love of his would be out
in next to no time, and whatever haven he might select must be
selected immediately. His eye, in a fine frenzy rolling, was caught
by the window of the Gardenia Tea Shoppe across the way. And
so keen was the sense of peril that gripped him that it now seemed
to have a kindly and a welcoming look.

There is this to be said for Tea Shoppes, no matter how
revolting to a dyspeptic man the wares in which they deal, that
in extending their hospitality they do not keep their eye on the
clock. At a bespoke tailor's, to take an instance at random, the
cry is all for rapid action. You dash in, bespeak your bit of
tailoring and dash out again. You can't make it too quick for the
tailor. If you take a seat and show signs of settling down for the
evening, he raises his eyebrows. But in a Tea Shoppe you can
linger. And Mr. Duff's primary requisite was a place where he
could linger till the All Clear had been blown. He was across
the street and through the door and panting in a wickerwork chair
almost before he knew he had started.

The ladylike waitress greeted him in surprise.

"Hello! Forgotten something?"

"Gimme some tea."

"Tea?"

"And buns."

"Yes, sir," said the waitress, with a new respect and approval
in her voice. There had been a time when she had looked a little
askance at Mr. Duff, not liking his offhand manner towards that
fancy cake, but now all was forgiven. A man of the right sort,
obviously. She could recall no previous case of a client liking his
meal so much that he immediately returned for another. A notable
compliment for the Gardenia's catering.

She went off to give the order in a modest flutter of excitement,
and Mr. Duff with a sigh of relief leaned back in his chair.

But even now his troubled spirit was not to be at rest. There
spoke from behind him a feminine voice, and he swung round,

blinking. It seemed to him that life this afternoon had been just one damned feminine voice after another.

"Why, how do you do?" said the voice, and he perceived, sitting at the next table, Vera Pym, the Rose and Crown's efficient barmaid.

Vera Pym had come to the Gardenia Tea Shoppe to brood and ponder. Pique at his aggravating behaviour had, of course, been partly responsible for her calling Chibnall up on the telephone that morning and regretting her inability to take tea with him in his pantry owing to an unfortunate previous engagement, but in any case she would have preferred to be alone. She wanted to give her whole mind to the problem of Mr. Duff's moustache. There must, she felt, if she thought long enough, be some way of discovering once and for all if it was false or genuine.

His abrupt incursion had for an instant alarmed her. Then she had fought down her momentary panic with a barmaid's splendid resolution. There is good stuff in Britain's barmaids, and the Motherland points at them with justifiable pride. This, she told herself, was just what a conscientious investigator would have wished to happen. To fraternize as much as possible with suspects, thus lulling them to a false security and learning their secrets, is the aim of every detective whose heart is really in his work.

So she said "Why, how do you do?" and tried not to shudder. The moustache, seen close to, looked more villainous than ever; and in addition to this the man's features were working violently, as if in almost ungovernable rage. As always when in the presence of the other sex, Mr. Duff had started making faces.

"Well, you're just in time to give me tea," she said, with the brightness which her professional training enabled her to put at will like a garment. "I'll come over to your table, shall I?"

In normal circumstances, Mr. Duff would have answered this question with an unhesitating negative. But now he found himself at a loss. Short of rising and leaving the Tea Shoppe, it seemed to him that he was helpless against this woman's advances. And a glance out of the window showed him how Utopian any dream of rising and leaving would be. Mrs. Chavender had just some out of the Rose and Crown and was standing on the pavement, waiting for her Pekinese to finish sniffing at a banana skin.

"They're getting me some tea and buns," said Miss Pym.

"They're getting *me* some tea and buns," said Mr. Duff.

"Well, that's splendid, isn't it?" said Miss Pym.

"Great," said Mr. Duff, and sat back feeling like somebody in one of his companion's favourite works of fiction who has been trapped by one-eyed Chinamen in a ruined mill.

Conversation flagged for a while. It is never easy to know just what to say to the criminal classes, and Miss Pym found herself short of small-talk. But presently the return of the waitress, preceded by a revolting smell of hot buns, emboldened her to continue. She poured out tea for herself and host, and moved her own cup as far away from him as was possible. She had known too many men who dropped mysterious white pellets in tea-cups to take any chances.

"Lovely day," she said.

"Ur," said Mr. Duff.

"I expect you were surprised to find me in here, weren't you?"

"Ur," said Mr. Duff.

"It's my afternoon off," explained Miss Pym.

"Ur," said Mr. Duff.

"It's nice to get away from that old bar once and again," proceeded Miss Pym, beginning to hit her stride. "Apart from the hard work of it all, there's the society. It gets very mixed, specially in the evenings, when the proletariat come in and play darts. I've often thought I'd sooner be a waitress in a place like this. More refinement. They give you a good tea here. Nice, these buns, aren't they?"

"Sure," said Mr. Duff, who had absent-mindedly swallowed one and could feel it fighting with the fancy cake and the double brandies preparatory to turning to lead inside him.

The monosyllable gave Miss Pym a cue. Your good detective is always on the alert to seize these opportunities of keeping the conversation going.

"You're an American gentleman, aren't you?"

"Yes."

"I thought so. The way you said 'Sure.' I can always tell Americans. But," said Miss Pym, who had had a good grounding in vaudeville comedy, "I can't tell them much. Ha, ha."

"Ha, ha," echoed Mr. Duff despondently. He looked out of the window again. Mrs. Chavender was still there. The Pekinese was now sniffing at a piece of paper.

"Mr. Chibnall sometimes talks of going to America. He says the salaries butlers get over there are literally fantastic."

"Mr. Chibnall?"

" My *fiancé*."

Mr. Duff perked up amazingly. In another distrait moment, not realizing what he was doing, he had swallowed a second bun, and it had teamed up with its predecessor, forming a solid *anschluss*, but the relief of discovering that this young woman was not as he had supposed an unattached siren, ready for any excesses, overcame his physical discomfort.

"Going to be married, are you?"

"When we've saved enough to buy a pub."

"They're expensive, I guess?"

"They run into money. But Sidney's a saving man, and I've put by a bit. Some of these commercials that come into my bar sometimes give you a good tip for the races. I had Westinghouse for the Ascot Gold Cup. A hundred to eight. That was ten pounds, right away."

"Well, well, well. You'll be a Hetty Green before you know where you are."

As is so often the way with a shy man, once the ice has been broken, Mr. Duff was beginning quite to enjoy this little adventure. Mrs. Chavender and Pekinese had now disappeared, but he felt no inclination to leave. He even ate another bun with something of a devil-may-care flourish.

"Who's she?"

"She was one of the richest women in America."

"I suppose everybody makes tons of money there?"

"Yes, and when they've made it, what happens? Does Mister Whiskers let 'em keep it? Not a hope. Listen," said Mr. Duff, beginning to swell, "lemme——"

He paused. He had been about to speak freely and forcefully of some of the defects of the existing Administration in his native country, but he felt that a *tête-à-tête* with a charming woman was not the occasion for it. Better to wait till he was back with the boys at the Union League Club.

"Plenty taxes in America these days," he said, condensing the gist of it into a sentence. He became aware that his guest was eyeing him intently. "Smatter?" he asked, puzzled.

"Pardon?"

"You seemed to be looking at me pretty hard."

Miss Pym simpered coyly.

"You'll think I'm awful, but I was admiring your moustache."

"Oh?"

"You don't often see American gentlemen with moustaches. Not big ones, Must have taken a lot of growing, if you don't mind me being personal."

"Oh, well," said Mr. Duff, with something of the air of a modest hero protesting that any man could have done what he had done.

"Mind if I look at it?"

"Go right ahead," said Mr. Duff, now not so much the modest hero as the big shot presenting some favoured visitor with the freedom of the city.

Miss Pym leaned forward. Her heart was thumping. She passed a shapely hand over the growth. And Chibnall, who had just arrived outside the window, halted abruptly and stood staring, a dark flush spreading slowly over his face.

That telephone call, with its airy allusions to previous engagements, had left Chibnall in a frenzy of doubt and suspicion. A bystander who had heard his careless "Oh? Right ho. Well, see you some time" would not have divined it, but his soul had seethed like a cistern struck by a thunderbolt. Something, he felt, was up. And it was in order to ascertain, if possible, what this something was that he had hastened to Loose Chippings.

Hoping against hope that the woman he loved was merely taking tea with the wife of the Rose and Crown's landlord, as she did from time to time, he had first gone there to enquire, and had been informed that Miss Pym had been seen stepping across the way to the Gardenia. And here in the Gardenia she was, carousing with the moustached visitor at the inn, whom she had so cunningly affected to distrust and dislike—and not only carousing, but actually patting his face.

It was, in short, the black business of the commercial traveller over again, only worse, far worse. There could be no question here of professional gestures designed to stimulate trade. And it was a long step from straightening ties to patting faces. This, felt Chibnall, was a straight orgy, and something like it, he told himself, was precisely what he had been expecting.

Clenching his fists till the knuckles stood out white under the strain, Sidney Chibnall drew back into the doorway of a ham and beef shop to think it over.

Inside the Gardenia, Miss Pym had concluded her investigations. It was just as she had suspected. Her fingers, roaming lightly through the jungle, had touched a hard substance which could be nothing but glue or spirit gum or whatever it was that the Underworld employed when disguising its upper lip with hair.

She rose. It was imperative that she telephone Chibnall about this immediately. All that a woman could do she had done, and it was now time for the tougher male to take over.

"Yes, it's beautiful," she said, panting a little, like a girl who has discovered a dismembered corpse in the attic. "Lovely. Well, I must be shoving along. Ta for the tea."

She hurried out, it seemed to Mr. Duff a trifle abruptly, and after pausing to pay the bill he also left. And he had scarcely set foot on the pavement, when he had the identical experience which had happened to him on the previous morning. There fell suddenly upon his shoulder a heavy hand.

The only detail which differentiated the two episodes was the circumstance that this second heavy-hander was a good deal better looking than his predecessor had been. Yesterday, Mr. Duff had found himself staring at a squashed nose and aeroplane ears. To-day, it was on a handsome, clean-cut face that his attention was riveted. But this was not really so much of an improvement as it sounds, for the face was suffused with violent emotion and only the dullest observer could have failed to note that the glitter in the eyes was homicidal.

It would have shocked Mrs. Steptoe profoundly, could she have known that her butler was capable of looking like that. She would also have disapproved of the way he spoke.

"Oi!" he said.

"Ouch!" said Mr. Duff.

"Just a minute," said Chibnall.

"What the devil are you doing?" said Mr. Duff.

"I'll tell you what I'm going to do," said Chibnall, swift with the effective repartee. "I'm going to knock your ugly fat head off and dance on it."

"Why?" asked Mr. Duff, not unreasonably.

"You don't know, do you?" said Chibnall, and brought his teeth together with an unpleasant click. "Ha! He doesn't know!"

There had been a time, in the hammer-throwing days of his youth, when J. B. Duff would have had a short way with this sort of thing. But the years, bringing with them surplus material about the waistline, had brought also pusillanimity and the instinct for self-preservation. He found himself with little appetite for a vulgar brawl. This apparent lunatic had a hard, athletic look, and he himself had not only allowed his muscles to grow flaccid but was at the moment full to the brim with tea and buns.

The ladylike waitress was beginning to get used to Mr. Duff. She showed scarcely any surprise as he now re-entered the Gardenia Tea Shoppe, moving extraordinarily well for a man of his years. He had become an old customer, a sort of foundation member, and she beamed on him as such.

"More tea?" she said brightly.

Mr. Duff sank into a chair with a corroborative nod.

"And buns?"

"Yup."

The waitress was looking like a preacher at a revival meeting who watches the sinners' bench filling up. If there were more men in it like Mr. Duff, her eye seemed to say, the world would be a better place.

"Very good, sir. Is this gentleman with you?" she asked looking past him. "Why, it's Mr. Chibnall. Good evening, Mr. Chibnall."

"Good evening."

"Lovely weather."

"Beautiful," said the butler absently. He had halted at Mr. Duff's table, and was glowering down at him in a hostile and intimidating manner. It was with considerable relief that Mr. Duff realized that for the moment he proposed to go no further than glowering. He applauded the decent respect for the amenities which restrained the other from defiling these refined premises with anything in the nature of a rough house.

The waitress continued chatty.

"Your young lady's only just left, Mr. Chibnall."

"I saw her."

"She was having tea with this gentleman."

"I saw her."

His unresponsiveness had its effect.

"Well, I'll go and get your tea and buns," said the waitress, and went off to do so.

Chibnall leaned on the table. His aspect, in addition to being homicidal, now betrayed baffled fury. He was blaming himself for having relaxed his grip on Mr. Duff's shoulder, thus enabling the latter to get away and seek sanctuary. What he had popped in for now was to point out that this sanctuary must not be regarded as permanent.

"I'll be waiting for you outside," he said, to make this clear.

Mr. Duff did not speak. His intelligent mind, assisted by the waitress's recent remarks, had gathered now the reason for this man's at first inexplicable behaviour, and his heart sank as he realized how impossible it would be to explain. Nothing could alter the fact that he had been entertaining the other's *fiancée* to a dish of tea, and in this world one is judged by one's actions, not by one's purity of heart.

"Understand?"

"There," said the waitress in a motherly way, returning with a laden tray. "There you are."

"You won't see me," said Chibnall, "but I'll be there."

He strode from the shop. The waitress's eyes followed him admiringly.

"That was Mr. Chibnall," she said. "The butler at the Hall."

"Oh?" said Mr. Duff.

"Fine, strapping fellow, isn't he? It's funny, I always used to think of butlers as fat old men, always drinking port, but Mr. Chibnall is a mass of muscle."

"Ah?" said Mr. Duff.

"And the best boxer round these parts, they tell me. He beats them all at the Lads' Club. Strong as a lion, I'm told, and as quick on his feet as a panther. You aren't eating your buns."

"I'm not so sure I want them."

"Then I'll bring you some French pastry and assorted cakes," said the waitress, indulgently, like one humouring a spoiled child at a school treat. "Those ones with the cream and pink sugar on the top are the sort you like, aren't they?"

Vera Pym was coming away from the telephone booth, annoyed to learn that the man she sought was not on the premises of Claines Hall, when Chibnall entered the Rose and Crown. She saw him and ran to him, her copper-coloured hair dancing with excitement.

"There you are! I've just been trying to get you on the phone."

She looked about her, and saw that they were alone. "Sidney, it's true!"

"A fat lot more than you are," said Chibnall morosely.

"What do you mean?"

"I saw you."

"When?"

"Just now. In the tea-shop. With that fellow."

Miss Pym's attractive eyes widened.

"You don't mean you didn't understand?"

"I certainly did," said Chibnall. "Only too well." He laughed a hollow laugh. "And you pretending he was a crook!"

"But he is. That's why I was having tea with him. I wanted to make sure. I was in there by myself, thinking everything over, and suddenly there he was at the next table. Well, I knew I should never have such a good chance again, so I went and sat with him."

"You patted his face."

"I never. I was feeling his moustache."

"It's the same thing."

"It's not. Sidney, it's fastened on with glue!"

"What!"

"Yes."

"You really mean that?"

"I felt it."

"I mean, you weren't flirting with him?"

"Well, the idea! I was detecting him."

Chibnall relaxed. He had been looking like King Arthur interviewing Guinevere in the monastery. He now looked merely like a butler who has had a weight taken off his mind.

"So that was it!"

"Of course it was. Sidney, I've just remembered something. Sidney, do you know what? Yesterday morning, before you came into my bar, he had been asking the way to the Hall!"

"You don't mean it?"

"That's what he had. And didn't you hear that Weatherby fellow say his face was familiar? And didn't Weatherby leave just after he did? I see it all. They're pals. It's as plain as the nose on your face. Weatherby worms his way into the house, and then he lets this chap in at dead of night to burgle all the valuables."

"I wonder."

"It's what's known as working the inside stand."

"I believe you're right, Vera. I was thinking things over last night, and I came round to your view that there's something very fishy about that Weatherby. I don't like the way he's acting. He was prowling last night. Looking for nightingales, *he* said. But I don't know about him and this fellow with the moustache being pals. Wouldn't he have known him?"

"Not if he's put the moustache on since they plotted together, he wouldn't. You take my advice, Sidney, and watch Weatherby like a hawk. Pretty silly you'd look if you suddenly found him murdering you in your bed."

Chibnall flushed. His pride was touched.

"I'd like to catch him murdering me in my bed. Feel that," he said, directing her attention to a biceps strengthened to steely hardness by morning exercises and evening boxing at the Lads' Club.

"A lot of use that would be against a tommy gun."

"He hasn't got a tommy gun."

"How do you know he hasn't? You didn't see him unpack. You be careful, that's what I say."

"I will."

"And if he offers you any more of his tainted gold, you refuse it."

"Would you go so far as that?" said Chibnall dubiously.

In the Gardenia Tea Shoppe, J. B. Duff had unfastened the last three buttons of his waistcoat and was leaning back in his chair, breathing stertorously. Under the vigilant eye of the waitress, he had long since finished the French pastry, and she was now bringing him some more fancy cakes. He stared bleakly into a dark future. There would be a heavy price to pay for this—physical as well as financial.

But you cannot go into a Tea Shoppe and just sit. Nor, if a berserk butler is waiting for you outside, can you leave.

The waitress came back with the fancy cakes. It was plain from her somewhat abstracted manner that she had now come to look upon herself rather in the light of an experimental scientist and upon her customer as a guinea-pig.

"I'll tell you what," she said, struck with an idea. "After you've finished those, I'll get the cook to do you up some of her pancakes. Shall I?"

"Okay," said Mr. Duff, in a low voice, but not so low that his stomach was not able to overhear the word. It gave an apprehensive leap, and cowered miserably. Nothing could surprise it now. It had long since given up trying to understand what was going on in the front office.

THE afternoon of the garden party, that red-letter day for the nobility and gentry of Sussex, found Sidney Chibnall groaning in spirit.

There are moments in the life of every butler when he is compelled to wonder if flesh and blood can stand the demands made upon them or if they will not be forced to crack beneath the strain, and one of these comes when he holds office under a nervous hostess who is about to give her first important garden party. Chibnall was a man who took a pride in not sparing himself, but by lunch-time on the day of Mrs. Steptoe's colossal binge the constant ringing of the bell and the agitated enquiries of his employer as to whether all was well concerning the band, the refreshments, the extra help and the like had begun to take their toll.

These, however, were but the normal anxieties unavoidable at such a time. In addition to them, there weighed upon his mind the dark menace of the man Weatherby. Joss, he was convinced, intended to start something. And it was the thought of what an admirable opportunity he would have of doing so, with everybody in the place busy out in the grounds, that was causing Chibnall to groan in spirit. It is only when he has a big garden party on his hands and knows that during that garden party a Mayfair Man will be roaming the house with no check upon his movements that a butler really drains the bitter cup.

The comparative relaxation afforded by luncheon and a couple of quick ones in his pantry at the conclusion of the meal enabled his active brain to hit on a solution of his difficulties. It was with a clever and well-formulated scheme in his mind that he approached Mrs. Steptoe as she stood fidgeting on the terrace, watching the sky. Mrs. Steptoe had just discovered that she did not like the look of that sky.

"Well, Chibnall?"

"Might I have a word, madam?"

"There's a cloud over those trees there."

"Yes, madam."

"Oh, gosh!" cried Mrs. Steptoe emotionally. "And in another minute, I suppose, one might as well be standing under Niagara Falls. I'd like to find the man who invented this English climate and tell him what I think of him. Well, what is it?"

"It is with reference to the young man Weatherby, madam."

"What's he done now?"

"It is rather what he may do in the course of the afternoon that is causing me uneasiness, madam. I confess that I feel dubious about leaving him in occupation of the house while I and my staff are away from it."

His quiet impressiveness was not without its effect. Mrs. Steptoe removed a troubled eye from the cloud, which was now spreading across the sky like an ink stain.

"You really think he's a crook?"

"I am convinced of it, madam."

"Then what's to be done?"

"What I would advise, madam, is that you instruct me to go to him and inform him that you wish him to help with the service at the garden party. He will thus fully be occupied under my personal eye."

"Bright," said Mrs. Steptoe. "Very bright. More," she added, relapsing into gloom again, "than the weather is. It's going to pour down in a minute. Then what?"

"I fear you will be compelled to receive your guests in the drawing-room, madam."

"And a nice flop that will be. Not that I suppose anyone'll come if the county's under water. You ever been in California, Chibnall?"

"No, madam. I have never visited the United States of America, though I have often felt a desire to do so."

"What a Paradise!"

"So I was given to understand, madam, by a Californian gentleman whom I once met in a milk bar in London. He spoke extremely highly of his native state."

"You know what happens in California? You say to yourself: 'I feel like throwing a party. I'll have it in my garden two weeks from next Tuesday,' and you send out the invitations. You don't say: 'Will it be fine?' You know it'll be fine. You don't even have to wonder about it. But here . . . All right, go tell Weatherby."

The process of telling Weatherby occupied three minutes of

the butler's time. At the end of that period, he was back on the
terrace.

"I have seen the young man, madam."

"Then everything's all right?"

"No, madam. He refuses to assist with the service."

"What!"

"Yes, madam. I informed him of your wishes, but he merely
made some frivolous reply about the rules of the Valets' Union.
No such organization exists."

"Well, of all the . . . Listen, you go right back and tell him
from me——"

Mrs. Steptoe broke off. She had been on the point of requesting
her butler to tell Joss from her that his term of service beneath
the roof of Claines Hall was at an end and that he could get out
and stay out, but even as she started to speak there emerged
from the house a Vision. It was as if one of those full-page
coloured advertisements of what the well-dressed man is wearing
had detached itself from a monthly magazine and come on to
the terrace.

From the suède shoes on his large, flat feet to the jaunty hat
on his pumpkin-shaped head, Howard Steptoe was correct in
every detail. Birds twittered in admiration of his quiet grey suit,
bees drew in their breath sharply as they eyed that faultless shirt,
beetles directed one another's attention to the gardenia in the
buttonhole. And Mrs. Steptoe, who had been expecting something that looked like a tramp cyclist, revised her views about
dispensing with Joss's services. He might be a criminal, and as
fresh a criminal as ever wisecracked with one hand while pocket-
ing the spoons with the other, but to a man who could turn
Howard Steptoe out like that all must be forgiven.

"No, never mind," she said.

At this moment, it began to rain.

Joss was in the servants' hall, whiling away the time with a
crossword puzzle. If Chibnall had been gifted with second sight,
he could not have predicted more exactly this young man's plans
for the afternoon. It was his intention to wait till the house was
empty and then carry through the commission he had undertaken
on Mr. Duff's behalf. He realized now that in attempting that
night foray he had been foolishly blind to the advantages
offered to the young portrait-stealer by a garden party.

It was as he sat wondering what was the earliest hour at which he might reasonably expect the residents and guests at Claines Hall to have become stupefied by tea and cucumber sandwiches that he became aware of Chibnall brooding over him like a thundercloud.

"Ah, Chibnall," he said genially.

The butler's manner was cold.

"Mr. Steptoe wants you."

"You mean Mrs. Steptoe?"

"I mean Mr. Steptoe. He's in his room."

"Or, rather, on the lawn?"

"In his *room*," said Chibnall, raising his voice. "If you'd bothered to look out of the window, you'd have seen it's raining cats and dogs."

Joss directed his gaze at the window, and found the statement correct.

"Egad, so it is. I'm afraid this has messed up the garden party to some extent."

Chibnall had not intended to be chatty, but the topic which had been broached was one on which he felt so strongly that he was forced to say a word or two.

"Ruined. Half the guests have telephoned to say they aren't coming, and the ones that have come are squashed into the drawing-room. And is Mrs. Steptoe in a state!"

"I can readily imagine it," said Joss sympathetically. "It must have stuck the gaff into her up to the hilt. The heart bleeds. So Pop Steptoe has sneaked off to his room, has he? That won't do. His place is in the forefront of the battle. I'll go and shoo him back."

Complete though his confidence had been both in Charles the footman's judgment in the matter of gala wear and in Mr. Steptoe's docile acceptance of the clothes laid out for him, his employer's appearance smote Joss like a blow.

"Steptoe!" he cried, stunned with admiration. "My God! You look like Great Lovers Through the Ages!"

Mr. Steptoe was in no mood for compliments, however deserved.

"Listen," he said.

"I was wondering when you were going to say that."

"Listen," said Mr. Steptoe. "I'm in a spot." His manner was agitated in the extreme. He plucked nervously at his gardenia.

"Listen," he said. "Aren't you ever going to get around to swiping that portrait?"

"I'm biding my time."

"Well, don't. Do it now. I'm in a spot."

"So I understood you to say. What has happened?"

Mr. Steptoe advanced his lips to Joss's ear, and spoke in a hissing whisper.

"Listen," he said.

"Well?" said Joss, removing the ear and drying it.

"Listen. I did as you said. I grab me a bunch of those guys, and I take them around the corner and we shoot craps."

"Excellent."

"What do you mean, excellent? They cleaned me out."

"Cleaned you out?"

"That's what they did. There was a little bozo with pimples—a Baronet or something like that—that never stopped pulling out sevens and elevens. I couldn't get started. He come away all loaded down with my IOU's, and I've told him I'll send over the dough to-morrow. And if I don't come through, then what? He spreads it around among his gang, and the first thing you know Mrs. Steptoe has got the story. Cheese!" said Mr. Steptoe, shivering.

"What would she do?"

"Plenty."

"Then I agree with you. There must be no delay. I confess I had anticipated doing the job at a moment when the house was empty, but I don't suppose anyone will come into the breakfast-room."

"They're all having tea."

"That'll hold them. May I borrow your manicure set?"

"Eh?"

"I shall need scissors."

"I haven't any scissors."

"Then give me a razor blade."

A razor blade is not the ideal instrument for removing a canvas from its frame, but Joss made it serve. His task completed, he stood for a moment wondering whether to leave by the door and go to his room or by the French windows and make straight for the Rose and Crown. A rattle of rain against the glass decided him in favour of the former course. He looked up and down the passage. Nothing was stirring. He ran silently up the stairs, and

Sally, who had been sent by Mrs. Steptoe to her bedroom to fetch her wrist-watch, came out on to the landing just as he reached it.

"Oh!" said Sally.

"Ah!" said Joss.

"You made me jump."

"It was your guilty conscience that made you jump," said Joss sternly. "You're just the girl I was looking for, young S. Fairmile. I've been wanting a word with you for days. One very serious drawback to this place is that it's so difficult to get hold of you for a chat."

"Was there something particular you wanted to chat about?"

"There was. The time has come for a frank round table conference. In here, if you please."

"But this is Mrs. Steptoe's bedroom."

"That's fine," said Joss. "Nice and quiet."

★ 15 ★

H_E shut the door.

"Now, then," he said, "what's all this nonsense I hear about you being engaged?"

If a criticism could have been made of the tone in which he spoke it was that it resembled rather too closely that of a governess of rigid ethical views addressing one of her young charges upon whom suspicion of stealing jam has rested, and Sally gave a little gasp. Her full height was not much, but, such as it was, she drew herself to it. She had decided that cold dignity was what the situation demanded.

"I beg your pardon?"

"And well you may, if it's true. Is it true?"

"Perfectly true. May I ask what business it is of yours?"

"That," said Joss, more like a governess than ever, "is one of the silliest questions I ever heard. Considering that I'm going to marry you myself."

"Oh? I didn't know that."

"Well, you know it now. Why, good Lord, we were made for each other. I spotted it the minute you came into J. B. Duff's office. You don't mean you didn't get it, too? Why, it stuck out a mile. There were you, and there was I, and there we were, so to speak. My poor young fathead, I should have thought you would have got on to it right away."

Sally, who had relaxed, for it is a strain on the muscles drawing yourself to your full height, drew herself to her full height again.

"We are not amused," she said coldly.

"I beg your pardon?"

"I was merely trying to point out that you are not being a bit funny."

Joss stared.

"Funny? Of course I'm not being funny. What on earth would I want to be funny for?"

"Do you really want me to believe that you are serious?"

"Of course I'm serious."

"You realize, I suppose, that you've only seen me twice in your life?"

"Three times—and once would have been ample. What did you think I meant by all those hints I dropped about falling in love at first sight? People do fall in love at first sight, don't they? Look at Romeo. Look at Chibnall. He went into the Rose and Crown one morning, a heartfree butler with not a thing on his mind, except the thought of the pot of beer he was going to order, and there was a girl with copper-coloured hair behind the bar, and their eyes met, and it seemed to Chibnall as if something had gone all over him like. 'That's the one!' he said to himself, and that's what I said when you came into J. B. Duff's office. I knew in an instant that we had been destined for one another since the beginning of time. I loved you the moment I saw you. I worshipped you. I had been dreaming about you for years. I knew you would be along sooner or later. And in you came."

Sally was conscious of a strange breathlessness. This man might have a peculiar way of laying bare his heart, but she did not question his sincerity. Not even the fact that he had just wandered to Mrs. Steptoe's dressing-table and was absently drawing a face on the mirror with lipstick caused her to revise this opinion. Romeo and Chibnall might not have chosen this moment for drawing faces on mirrors, but this was Joss Weatherby, an incalculable being, for whom she was suddenly aware that she felt a very warm affection—of, she was careful to tell herself, a purely maternal nature.

"You'd better rub that out," she said.

"True," said Joss, doing so. "Well, that's the set-up."

There was a silence. Joss had found a jar of cold cream, and was applying it thoughtfully to the tip of his nose.

"I'm sorry," said Sally.

"Nothing to be sorry about. It's wonderful. When you consider what the odds are against your meeting the one person in the world who's intended for you, the thing's a miracle. Suppose you hadn't come to J.B.'s office that morning. Suppose I hadn't been there. Why, it's a pure fluke that I happen to be in England at all."

"I mean, I'm sorry you feel like that."

"Why?"

Something of her maternal warmth left Sally, to be replaced by a touch of resentment she had felt at the beginning of the interview. At times such as this, a girl likes to be helped out.

"Well, if you think I enjoy having to tell you that I'm in love with someone else——"

Joss gaped.

"You don't mean——"

"You've got cold cream all over your nose."

"You don't mean you're taking this engagement of yours seriously?"

"Don't you think engagements ought to be taken seriously?"

"Not this one."

"Oh?"

"Certainly not. The whole thing's absurd. It stands to reason that you can't really love this fellow."

"Do you know George?"

"Is his name George? No, I don't. But I know all about him. I've made enquiries in the servants' hall. He's a crooner. This is a known fact. He sings *Trees*. It's sheer nonsense to say you love him."

There had been a moment, when she had woken to the realization that she was engaged to be married, when Sally had been conscious of misgivings on this point herself. Lord Holbeton, as Joss had said, was addicted to singing *Trees*, and he had been doing it just before he proposed. Like so many *Trees*-singers, he always extracted the last drop of syrup from words and music, and that night he had let it go in a manner that might have melted a Medusa. Even Mr. Steptoe had seemed affected. And some malignant imp of doubt had whispered to her, as she lay thinking in bed next morning, that her acceptance of his proposal might have been merely an impulsive girl's natural reaction to a tenor voice that sounded like a swooning mosquito.

These misgivings had passed as quickly as they had come, but the fact that she had entertained them, if only for an instant, lent vehemence to her statement of faith now.

"I do!"

Joss was telling himself that he must be very tactful, very diplomatic.

"But the man's a mess," he said, in pursuance of this policy.

"He is not!"

"Well, no," said Joss, ever fair-minded, "I oughtn't to have said that. I know nothing against him, except that he sings *Trees*. I suppose it's just the idea of the girl you love even considering anyone else that's so revolting. It seems to go right against one's better nature. Very well, we'll let it go that he's quite a good chap in his way, and if he marries somebody else I am perfectly willing to send him a fish slice. But it's ridiculous to think of him marrying you. The thing doesn't make sense. And you're utterly mistaken in supposing that you love him. Dismiss that notion absolutely. Of course," said Joss, "one can see how you got the idea."

"Do tell me that."

"It's obvious. You were having a rotten time here. You were crushed and oppressed by old Ma Steptoe. It was 'Sally this' and 'Sally that.' 'Comb this dog! See that cook——' "

"That sounds like a bit out of *Old Man River*."

"You are familiar with *Old Man River*?"

"I am."

"I sing it a good deal."

"It must sound wonderful."

"It does. And there," said Joss, seizing on the point with the skill of a practical debater, "you have in a nutshell the essential difference between this George of yours and me. When I sing, I sing openly and honestly, starting from the soles of the feet, very deep and loud and manly, so that anyone can see that my heart is in the right place. He gives it out from the eyebrows in an effeminate trickle. The State rests."

"You were saying something about dogs and cooks."

"Oh, yes. I was just pointing out that your lot in the home was such a hard one that quite naturally you said to yourself 'Oh, hell! Anything to get out of this.' With the result that when George came along, you kidded yourself that you were in love with him."

This was so true that it stung Sally like the flick of a whip. However, long training as a poor relation had given her the ability to curb her temper in trying circumstances.

"I must be going," she said.

"Where?"

"Back to the drawing-room."

"Not before we've got all this threshed out. We can't leave it hanging in the air. It beats me why I can't make you see how things are between us. You must believe in affinities?"

"Like George and me?"

"Don't," pleaded Joss, "be funny at a moment like this. It clouds the issue. It isn't possible, I repeat, that you love this bird Holbeton. We know him in the servants' hall as That Bloke With The Adam's Apple.''

Sally had long since come to the conclusion that cold dignity was too difficult. She now found resentment equally hard to achieve. From their first meeting, she had been strangely drawn to this extraordinary young man, and her subconscious self was even now trying rather austerely to draw her attention to the fact that she was deriving far too much pleasure from his society at this moment.

Of course, it was abominable what he was saying about poor George, but there was no getting away from it that That Bloke With The Adam's Apple was an admirable description of him— terse, neat and telling the story in a sentence.

"Watch that Adam's apple. That's all I say. Watch it. And in the privacy of your chamber reflect what it would be like to spend the remainder of your life with it."

Nor was there any getting away from the fact that in Joss's company she felt stimulated and happy, as if she were a child watching a three-ring circus. That was how she had felt directly she had seen him, that first morning when they had drunk sherry together in the office of J. B. Duff.

A sudden, uncontrollable giggle escaped her.

"No laughing matter," said Joss reprovingly. "It would drive me nuts."

"I was thinking," Sally explained, "of Mr. Duff and the sherry."

Joss's stern face relaxed into a smile.

"Quite a party that."

"Quite."

"When he suddenly appeared from nowhere, shouting 'Hey!' I wonder if you experienced the same odd sensation that I did, as if the top of the head had parted abruptly from its moorings?"

"Yes, that's just how I felt."

"Twin souls," said Joss. "Twin souls. Two minds with but a single thought. But let us not diverge from the main theme. By Jove, though," he went on, "we haven't. J. B. Duff. We will now speak of him. I saw him yesterday."

"I did, too."

"So he said. And he told me something that shocked me. It appears that this delusion of yours that you love George Holbeton persists so strongly that you are prepared to steal portraits in order to get money for him so that he can marry you."

"Quite true."

"Well, thank Heaven, I can block that punt."

"You think so?"

"I know so."

"Oh?"

"Yes."

"Well, we needn't wrangle about it. He told me you were after the portrait too. Let the best man win."

"He has. I've got it."

"What."

"Under my waistcoat at this very moment, like a chest protector."

"I don't believe you."

"Well, look."

Sally uttered a wailing cry.

"Mr. Weatherby!"

"You may call me Joss."

"Joss, give it to me!"

"Thereby enabling you to marry a man who sings *Trees* at the drop of the hat? No, no. This is not the true Sally Fairmile speaking. This is a Sally Fairmile who has not yet come out from under the ether and is not responsible for what she says. Gosh, you'll thank me for this some day."

Desperation came upon Sally. She flung herself at him, like Mrs. Chavender's Pekinese attacking Mrs. Steptoe's Alsatian. Her fingers clawed at his waistcoat, and he caught her wrists. And then, so true is it that one thing leads to another and that you can try a good man just so high, he suddenly found that she was in his arms. After that, he hardly knew what he was doing. Chibnall, however, could have told him. Chibnall, with his intimate knowledge of the Nosegay Novelette series, would have recognized the procedure immediately. He was clasping Sally to his bosom and showering burning kisses on her upturned face.

This sort of thing went on for some time. It might have gone on longer, had not Lord Holbeton entered the room. Mrs. Steptoe, wearying of waiting for Sally to bring her that wrist-watch, had asked him if he would be kind enough to go and see what he could do about it.

★ 16 ★

THE spectacle at which Lord Holbeton found himself gazing was one which could not have been viewed with indifference by any *fiancé*. Owing to the noiseless manner in which he had opened the door, neither of the other two principals in the scene had become aware of his presence, and for some moments after his arrival what might be called the *status quo ante* continued to prevail. Joss was still kissing Sally, and Sally, who in the opening stages had kicked him on the shin, had just begun to realize that she was feeling disgracefully happy about it all.

That this was not the right attitude she was well aware. Her better self was being rather critical. Nevertheless, that was how she felt. In a curious sort of way this seemed to her something that ought to have happened long ago, something to which she had been looking forward without knowing it ever since that morning in Mr. Duff's office.

Lord Holbeton coughed.

"I say," he said.

The comment was one which to some might have seemed lacking in fire and spirit. It was not the sort of thing Othello would have said in similar circumstances. But the truth was that only with the greatest difficulty had the speaker managed to keep out of his voice a note of whole-hearted relief. The problem of how to find a way of cancelling his commitments without offending against the code of an English gentleman had been putting dark circles under his eyes. And now he perceived that it had been handed to him on a plate. Normally, the troth of a Holbeton, once plighted, would have had to stay plighted. But this altered everything.

In the time which had elapsed since he had proposed in the scented garden of Claines Hall, Lord Holbeton had been putting in some very intensive thinking, and he had come definitely to the conclusion that in becoming engaged to Sally Fairmile he had made a mistake. He liked Sally. He admired Sally. He wished her well and would watch her future career with considerable

130

interest. But, while still vague as to what exactly were the qualities which he demanded in a wife, he was very clear in his mind that she must not be the sort of girl who routs a man out at midnight to go and pinch portraits and gets him bitten in the leg by Pekinese.

"Look here," said Lord Holbeton.

Joss had released Sally. He would have preferred to go on showering burning kisses on her upturned face, but one has to do the civil thing. Now that her betrothed had put in an appearance, he could not be ignored. He must be drawn into their little circle.

"Oh, hullo," he said.

"Who are you?" said Lord Holbeton.

"Weatherby is the name."

"Why, dash it, you're Steptoe's man!"

"Yes."

"Well, I'm dashed. This won't do," said Lord Holbeton, for the first time addressing his remarks directly to Sally. "You can't do this sort of thing, you know. Go about hugging and kissing the domestic staff, I mean. I mean to say, dash it! Well, after this, of course, everything's off. This is official."

He strode from the room, without Mrs. Steptoe's wrist-watch.

On the part of at least one of the two occupants of the apartment the silence which he left behind him was a thoughtful one. Joss, as he returned to Mrs. Steptoe's dressing-table and started to draw a moustache on his upper lip with her mascara, was frowning meditatively. He realized now, what before had escaped his notice, that his recent behaviour was in certain respects open to criticism.

"I'm sorry," he said.

Sally did not speak. He peered into the mirror, hesitated whether to add a small imperial to the moustache, decided not to.

"You shouldn't have grappled with me. It put ideas into my head. Shall I go after him and explain?"

"No, don't bother."

Joss turned quickly. Sally gave a little squeal of laughter.

"Your face!"

"There is something wrong with it?"

"No, no. It's an improvement."

Joss was looking at her incredulously. He felt that he must have misunderstood her.

"Did you say 'Don't bother'?"

"I did."

"You don't want me to explain?"

"No, thanks."

"But I've ruined your romance."

"I prefer it that way."

"You said you loved him."

"One changes one's mind."

Joss nodded understandingly.

"I see. So you took my advice and studied that Adam's apple? Very agile, was it not? Like some creature of the wild struggling to escape from a trap or snare. You see now how right I was."

"You're always right."

"I wonder."

"That's very modest of you. What makes you doubtful?"

"Well, you see, I thought . . . I had an idea . . . There was a time, if you remember, when I thought it might be possible that you would marry me. But, of course, after what has occurred . . . after this loathsome exhibition I've just been making of myself . . . now that you realize that I'm the sort of man who——"

"—Takes advantage of a helpless girl?"

"Exactly! Did you notice? I grabbed you—hugged you——"

"—Kissed me."

"Yes," cried Joss, his voice vibrating with indignation and abhorrence, "and kissed you. What a cad! What a hound! We don't want anything more to do with J. P. Weatherby after that."

"What does the P. stand for?"

"Parmalee."

"How frightful."

"Named after a godfather, and not a penny to show for it. No," said Joss, resuming his remarks, "that will be about all we shall require from J. P. Weatherby, I fancy. We wash him out. We dismiss him."

"So you can be wrong, after all."

"What do you mean?"

"If you don't know what I mean——"

"I do know what you mean, but I don't see how you can mean it. Sally, will you?"

"Parmalee, I will."

He clasped her in his arms, and went into his routine. Practice makes perfect. It was some time before he spoke again.

"This," he said, "is heaven!"

"Is it?"

"Yes," said Joss, "I do not mince my words. It's heaven." He paused. "Heaven," he repeated. "And yet——"

"—You wish it hadn't happened?"

"No, no, no, no, no, no, no," said Joss, with all the emphasis at his disposal. "What I was about to say was—— And yet I am weighed down by a sense of unworthiness."

"I thought you thought rather highly of J. P. Weatherby?"

"I do. I do. A splendid fellow. Nevertheless, I have this crushing sense of unworthiness. If someone came along at this moment and said 'Tell me, Weatherby, to settle a bet, what have you done to deserve this?' I should be nonplussed. I shouldn't know what to answer. I should just go all red and shuffle my feet. Because we've got to face it, I'm not fit to button your shoes."

"They lace."

"I've put up a front. Probably I have struck you as, if anything, a little on the brash side. But really I'm a crawling, creeping chunk of humility. I look at you, and I look at myself, and I feel like a swine-herd in a fairy story who finds himself loved by a princess. What you see in me, I can't imagine."

"Why, your looks. Your character. Your bright future."

"Is my future bright?"

"Glittering. You're going to take that portrait to Mr. Duff and get your job back."

"Better than that. It was a rotten job. All right for a young bachelor, but we men who are planning to marry and settle down have got to look ahead. I intend to stand out for being made head of the Art Department. Those are my terms," said Joss, and his voice was strong and resolute. "If J.B. won't meet them, not a smell of this portrait does he get."

"Oh, Joss, are you sure?"

"Sure?"

"That he wants it as much as that? It would be awful to spoil everything by asking too much."

"You wait. He'll come across. I know J.B. He's one of those men whose legs you have to count to be sure they aren't mules. When he gets an idea into his head, you couldn't dig it out with a chisel. He has set his heart on having this portrait, and the thing has become an obsession."

Sally was looking thoughtful.

"Something on your mind?" asked Joss.

"I was thinking that I ought to go and see him."

"Instead of me?"

"Yes. I can do it much better than you. You're not very tactful."

"Me? Not tactful?"

"You might throw him out of the room, or something."

"But you don't understand. This is a very intricate business deal, and I doubt if a slip of a girl is capable of handling it. It isn't only a question of my end of the thing. I represent a syndicate, whose interests must be borne in mind throughout the negotiations."

"I don't understand."

"I told you you didn't. Can you keep a secret?"

"I don't think so."

"Well, try to keep this one. Money, and substantial money, has got to pass between J. B. Duff and self. Mr. Steptoe needs his little bit. He wants to return to Hollywood and resume what appears to have been a highly promising career in the pictures."

"I didn't know he was in pictures."

"Extra work till just at the end, and then he was in one where he had three good speeches. Get him to tell you about it some time. And then . . . I wish I knew how good you were at giving an imitation of the silent tomb."

"Why?"

"Because what I am about to say must go no further, if that. Mrs. Chavender."

"What about her?"

"She wants her cut."

"Mrs. Chavender? But she has all the money there is."

"No. She had, but hasn't any longer. Lemme, as J.B. would say, tell you a little story."

"Have you heard him say that?"

"Dozens of times."

"He said it to me that day in his office."

"Oh? Well, to get back to it, lemme."

He held his audience. There was no question about that. Sally listened absorbed as the story of Mrs. Chavender's unfortunate circumstances unfolded itself.

"The poor old thing!"

" 'Poor' is the exact word."

"I see what she means. If Mrs. Steptoe knew, she would trample all over her."

"With spiked shoes."

"Of course she must have her money. I'll be very firm with Mr. Duff."

"You're sure you can manage it. You won't weaken?"

"Of course not."

"Very well. Here's the portrait. Tuck it into your shirt-front, and be very careful not to let anyone get you into a game of strip poker. Are you going to the Rose and Crown in your car?"

"Yes. I'll be back in no time."

"It will seem like hours. Where do we meet?"

"At the gate?"

"Right. Skin off your nose, Sally."

"Skin off yours, Joss."

The door closed. Joss sank into a chair. He drew up a small table and put his feet on it. He took out his pipe and lit it. This wonderful thing that had happened to him demanded quiet, steady meditation. He had to go over all that had occurred since he had met Sally, taking each moment by itself and savouring it like the leaf of an artichoke before going on to the next.

And he had just reached the point where he had found her in his arms, and was in the process of dwelling on this phase of their relationship with a tender, reminiscent smile, when his attention was attracted by a noise in his rear like an explosion of an ammunition dump, and he looked round to see Mrs. Steptoe. Like J. B. Duff on a similar occasion, equally historic, she was standing in the doorway, spellbound.

Although in Joss's demeanour, as he rose, an observer would have noted only a rather charming, old world courtliness, he was not without a certain apprehensiveness, a sort of nebulous feeling that this was not so good and that the going in the immediate future promised to be sticky. He had just discovered— or rediscovered—with so many other things to think about, it had temporarily slipped his mind—that this room in which he had been enjoying his reverie was Mrs. Steptoe's bedroom. Hard words, he feared, might be spoken and black looks be looked.

Nor had his intuition deceived him. If Fate had wished to cement a lasting friendship between this woman and himself, it could hardly have brought them together under less favourable conditions.

Even before opening the door, Mrs. Steptoe had been feeling a little edgy. The rain had ruined her garden party. She had had to spend the afternoon cooped up in a stuffy drawing-room with some of the dullest people she had ever met. The pimpled Baronet, laughing amusedly like one telling a good story which he knows is sure to be well received, had just revealed to her that her Howard had been yielding to his lower instincts and trying to take money off his guests at craps. And the more messengers she dispatched to fetch wrist-watches for her, the fewer wrist-watches did she get.

It just needed the sight of her husband's valet in her bedroom, wreathed in tobacco smoke with his feet on the table, to complete her day.

"*Well!*" she said.

There is really very little that a man can do at a moment like this, but something, Joss felt, might be accomplished by an apologetic smile. He released one, accordingly, and his companion quivered from head to foot as if he had struck her with a sandbag. There are certain situations, one of which had now arisen in Mrs. Steptoe's life, when a smile, however apologetic, seems to a woman the ultimate pay-off.

"Grinning!" she said in a strangled voice, not getting the spirit behind the smile at all. "I find him in my bedroom," she went on more loudly, as if confiding her grievances to a slightly deaf friend on whose sympathy she knew that she could rely. "I find him right plumb spang in the middle of my bed-room . . . smoking a pipe . . . his feet on the table . . . and he ger-RINS!"

"I assure you, madam——"

"GRINS!" said Mrs. Steptoe. "Like a half-witted ape," she added, specifying more exactly.

There seemed to Joss nothing to do in the circumstances but make wounded noises. He made them.

"Listen!" said Mrs. Steptoe, having probably picked up the expression from her mate.

She began to speak again, and now her voice, which at first had been hushed as if by a sort of awe, rang out like a clarion. And for some time Joss listened with bowed head as she touched on the numerous aspects of his character which did not appeal to her. Exactly when he began to feel that this nuisance must cease, he could not have said. But when the thought did come, it took root.

"Madam," he said, taking advantage of the fact that even an angry woman has sometimes to pause for breath, "I should be glad if you would accept my resignation. Dating from to-morrow."

"Resignation my foot!" said Mrs. Stiptoe, a puff of flame coming from her nostrils. "You're fired. Dating from to-day."

"Very good, madam. And now," said Joss, "if you will excuse me, I must be leaving you. I have an appointment."

Time, what with his thoughts and Mrs. Steptoe's conversation, had passed on such fleeting wings that he anticipated, as he made his way down the drive, that he might have to wait some little while at the tryst before Sally made her appearance. To his surprise, she was already there.

She seemed agitated.

"What a time you've been!"

"I'm sorry. I was chatting with Mrs. Steptoe. Difficult to get away. Well, everything all straight?"

"Joss! An awful thing has happened!"

"Eh?"

"I saw Mr. Duff."

"Well?"

"Joss, he doesn't want the portrait!"

"What!"

"He told me to take it back," said Sally, her voice rising to a wail.

Her stout heart failed her. She burst into tears.

★ 17 ★

IT is not the easiest of tasks to scoop a crying girl out from behind a steering-wheel and hoist her over the side and fold her in your arms and stanch her tears, but Joss managed it at length. The sobs became gurgles. The gurgles faded into silence.

"Now, then," he said. "Tell me all."

Sally gulped.

"I'm sorry. I was a fool."

"No, no. Nothing like a good cry. What seems to be the trouble?"

"I told you. He doesn't——"

"Yes, but there must be some mistake. You probably misunderstood him."

"I didn't. It's quite simple really, I suppose."

"Not to me."

"I mean, now that he's going to marry Mrs. Chavender——"

"What!"

"Yes. She went to see him at the inn this morning, and they arranged it then. He's been in love with her for years. Didn't he tell you?"

"No, he didn't mention that."

"And now that they are going to be married, of course he doesn't need her portrait. He only wanted it when he thought he had lost her for ever, so that he could have something to remember her by. I'm surprised he didn't tell you."

"Probably slipped his mind."

"But why did you think he wanted it?"

"Wouldn't anyone want a genuine Weatherby? But let's begin at the beginning. You arrived at the Rose and Crown and found him——"

"Sitting in the lounge. He looked very ill. Apparently he ate something that disagreed with him and had a bad attack of indigestion last night."

"Ah!"

"He told me he thought he was going to die. And this morning Mrs. Chavender came to see him."

"I'm beginning to understand. There he was, weak and wan after his night of suffering, and in walks Mrs. Chavender and gives aid and comfort. Is that right?"

"Yes. He says she was like a ministering angel."

"He swiped that from me. I once wrote a poem about woman being not so hot in our hours of ease but coming across in a big way when pain and anguish rack the brow. I suppose he got hold of a copy. Yes, I begin to follow the continuity. Mrs. Chavender comes into the sick-room, and starts being the ministering angel. He thinks of the old days and what might have been. She places a cool hand on his fevered forehead, and he takes it in his and says: 'Why did we ever part? Why, when we were on to a good thing, did we not push it along? Can we not make a new start?' She thinks the idea sound, and they fix it up. Something on those lines was what happened, I imagine."

"I suppose so."

"Indigestion is an amazing thing. It softens the toughest."

"But he had always loved her."

"I was forgetting that."

"It's sweet, of course."

"Oh, most sweet."

"But rather awkward for us."

"Yes, one was rather relying on delivery of that portrait to solve our little perplexities. Did you touch on me and my job?"

"Of course. I told him we were engaged."

"How did he seem to take it?"

"He said I was crazy and advised me to break it off."

"The lovable old gentleman!"

"He said he had understood that I wanted to marry George and that he had been thinking it over and had decided that he had misjudged George all these years. He said there was a lot of good in him."

"He must have been on an absolute toot last night. No ordinary attack of indigestion would sap the brain to that extent."

"He has given George his money."

"That's splendid news. I was worrying myself sick about George. And my job?"

"No."

"Off?"

"Yes. He said he had been thinking——"

"He thinks too much."

"—And he had come to the conclusion that it was having you around that gave him indigestion. He said he couldn't explain, but you did something to him."

"The old devil. I saved his life."

"Yes, I reminded him of that, and he said that he had put up with you for two years and he considered that that squared it. Did you make him drink brandy yesterday?"

"I didn't make him. I offered it, and he lapped it up. Why?"

"He said it was that that upset him. It seemed to rankle, rather."

"The mind of a man like J. B. Duff is unfathomable. I think that long association with hams must have unhinged his reason. Well, if he won't give me my job back, I'm afraid we may have to wait a little before we get married. I have nothing against love in a cottage, but just at the moment I don't see how it would even run to that. My capital is about fifteen pounds, and I am asking myself a little dubiously how it is to be augmented. Who wants an artist?"

"I do."

"Bless you, You're sure you wouldn't prefer to switch back to George, now that he has the stuff?"

"No, thanks."

"My God!" said Joss, struck by an unnerving thought. "Do you realize that if I hadn't overslept myself that morning, we should never have met?"

"Shouldn't we?"

"No. I was supposed to be at the office at ten. If I had got there on time, I should have been gone long before you arrived. But owing to having stayed up late, shooting craps, I didn't clock in till eleven. What a lesson this should teach to all of us."

"To shoot craps?"

"That, of course. But what I was really thinking of was how one ought never to be punctual. From now on, I shall make a point of always being at least an hour late for everything."

"Including the wedding?"

"The wedding. Ah! Now we're back to it. What do we do about that?"

"It's difficult, isn't it?"

"There must be some way. People are getting married every

day. They can't all be millionaires. I'll tell you what. Give me the canvas, and I'll hide it in my room, and then I'll go for a long walk and think things over. I get rather bright after I've been walking a mile or two. Expect to hear from me shortly."

The evening was well advanced when Joss returned to Claines Hall. The rain had stopped, and a belated sun was shining brightly. It had brought Lord Holbeton out into the grounds for a saunter before dinner.

Lord Holbeton was feeling in the pink. As he made his way down the drive, he walked on air. He was honourably free from an alliance which, as has been shown, he had come to recognize as entangling, and he had in his pocket a cheque bearing his trustee's signature. If that was not a pretty goodish day's work, George, second Baron Holbeton, would have been vastly interested to know what was.

He sang, as he floated along, naturally selecting his favourite melody, and he had just got as far as the line about nests of robins in the hair and was rendering it with even more than his customary *brio*, when there impinged upon his ears one of the gloomier passages of *Old Man River*, and he perceived coming towards him the bowed figure of the chap Weatherby.

When a man singing *Trees* meets a man singing *Old Man River*, something has to give. They cannot both continue to function. Lord Holbeton generously decided to be the one to yield. It gave him a slight pang not to be able to do the high, wobbly note on the "hair," but a man learns to take the rough with the smooth.

"Hullo," he said. "What ho."

In normal circumstances, he might not have been so expansive. But this evening he was the friend of all mankind.

For a moment, it seemed as if Joss, like Old Man River, would just keep rolling along. He was walking with bent head, his manner preoccupied. Then he appeared to realize that he had been addressed, and he halted.

"Oh, hullo."

It seemed to Lord Holbeton that the blighter looked a bit dejected, and he was not mistaken. His walk had brought Joss no solution of the problems confronting him. It had, indeed, merely deepened and intensified that unpleasant feeling, which comes to all of us at times, that he was in the soup and liable at any moment to sink without trace. He had endeavoured to be gay and debonair while discussing the future with Sally, but not for an instant had he lost sight of the fact that this future was a murky one.

"I say," said Lord Holbeton, "Sally's been telling me about you."

"Oh, yes?"

"She says you're not a man. I mean, not really a man. I mean," said Lord Holbeton, determined to make his meaning clear, "you only signed on with old Steptoe so as to be near her."

"Yes."

"Very creditable," said Lord Holbeton handsomely.

There was a pause. Joss, who had now been able to bring his mind to bear on these exchanges, was feeling somewhat embarrassed.

"She tells me you know old Duff."

"Yes."

"Served under his banner, and so forth."

"Yes."

"What an egg!"

"Yes."

"Rummy, if you come to think of it, that we never met. I mean, you constantly popping in and out of the office, and self repeatedly dropping in to try to gouge the old boy for a bit of the stuff, you'd have thought we'd have run into one another."

"Yes."

"Still, there it is."

"Yes."

It occurred to Joss that up to the present all this cordiality had been a little one-sided and that it was time for him to do his bit.

"I hear I have to congratulate you," he said.

"Eh?"

"Duff has given you your money, I'm told."

"Oh, I see. Yes, yes, oh yes. I couldn't think what you meant for a moment. Yes, I've got the cheque on my person now. I'm going to London after dinner, so as to be right on the spot tomorrow morning for paying-in purposes in case he changes his mind. I've had that happen to me before."

"Oh, yes?"

"Yes. When the old blister gets these spells of his, that's how it works. While weakened by the pangs, he's all mellowness and loving kindness. But comes a time when the reaction sets in, and then he's his old self again. And that's when you want to watch out. I remember a couple of years ago he went to a City dinner, and next morning he sent for me and told me he'd come to the conclusion that he had been misjudging me all these years and that there was really a lot of good in me. And, to cut a long story short, he tottered to his desk and wrote me out a cheque for the full amount. And, like an ass, I wasted the rest of the day going round and showing it to chaps and having my health drunk, and by the time I got to the bank next morning I found he'd had the bally thing stopped. Taught me a lesson, that, I can tell you. If anyone happens to ask you my whereabouts at nine a.m. to-morrow you can reply with perfect confidence that I'm standing on the steps of the City and Home Counties Bank, waiting for the establishment to open."

Joss was staring, open-mouthed.

"You don't mean that?"

"I do. Right on the top step."

"I mean, is that really what happens with J.B.?"

"Invariably."

"Then you think . . . Well, take a case. If, while under the influence, he thought he was in love with someone——"

"Old Duff?" said Lord Holbeton incredulously.

"I'm just taking the first instance that comes into my mind."

"I should be vastly surprised if even after a City dinner——"

"Just for the sake of argument. You think that later on, when he was feeling better, remorse would supervene?"

"Super what?"

"You think he would regret?"

"Oh, bitterly, beyond a question."

Something seemed to go off inside Joss like a spring. It was hope dawning.

"I must ponder on this," he said. "You have opened up a new line of thought."

"You going?"

"If you don't mind. I should like to meditate."

"Oh, rather," said Lord Holbeton, with a spacious wave of his hand, as if to indicate that he was free to do so wherever he pleased, all over the grounds. "Go ahead. Give my regards to Sally, if you see her."

Again there was a pause. Once more, Joss felt embarrassed. He could not forget that this was the man whom he had deprived of the only girl who could possibly matter to any man. True, the second Baron was not looking notably depressed, but that, he presumed, merely signified that he was wearing the mask, biting the bullet and keeping a stiff upper lip.

"I'm sorry," he said, awkwardly.

"Sorry?"

"About Sally and me."

"What, already?" said Lord Holbeton, surprised.

"I mean . . . I can understand how you must be feeling . . ."

"Oh, that?" said Lord Holbeton, comprehending. "My dear chap, don't give it another thought. I'm all right. I'm feeling fine. Once I've got that cheque safely deposited, I shan't have a care in the world. I shall go to Italy and have my voice trained. Best thing that could have happened, is my view of the matter. Nice girl, of course. None better. But personally I consider that a man's an ass to get married. Silly business altogether, I've decided."

It was a point which Joss would have liked to debate hotly, but he was unable to give his mind to it. Was that, he was asking himself, what J. B. Duff was feeling or shortly about to feel? He walked back to the house, and reaching the staff quarters found Chibnall at the telephone.

"Yes?" he was saying. " 'Oo? Weatherby? Yes, here he is. You're wanted on the telephone," said Chibnall, speaking coldly.

Joss took the instrument.

"Hullo?"

"Weatherby?"

"Yes."

"Listen. Can anybody hear?"

Joss looked round. He was alone.

"No."

"Then listen. Can you come here right away?"

"I dare say I could fit it in."

"Then listen. Go find that girl of yours, and get that portrait from her and bring it with you."

"You want it?"

"Of course I want it."

"You said you didn't."

"I've changed my mind."

"Oh?"

"Understand?"

"Perfectly."

"Then come along. And, listen," said Mr. Duff, "make it snappy."

18

I N fancying that he had sensed in Chibnall's manner at their recent encounter a certain coldness, Joss had not erred. The sound of Mr. Duff's voice over the wire had shocked the butler to his foundations. Brief though their conversation in the Gardenia Tea Shoppe had been, he had recognized it immediately: and it was with a feeling that now was the time for all good men to come to the aid of the party that he had handed over the instrument. The thought that two of the Underworld are using his employer's telephone for the hatching of their low plots can never be an agreeable one to a zealous butler.

As always when he had solid thinking to do, he had made his way to the cell-like seclusion of his pantry. The servants' hall, with its flow of merry quip and flashing badinage, he reserved for his more convivial moments when he was in the mood for the gay whirl. He poured himself out a glass of port, and sat down to ponder.

Stern though his determination was to foil whatever foul designs this precious pair might be meditating, there was mingled with it a touch of resentment. It seemed unjust to him that a man who was paid for buttling should be compelled to throw in gratis, as a sort of bonus to his employer, the unremitting efforts of a secret service man and a highly trained watch-dog. It was quite possible that the man Weatherby and his associate were planning some lightning stroke in the night, and that would mean sitting up again. Reflecting how much he liked his sleep and how cramped he had felt after that last vigil, Chibnall almost regretted that he was so conscientious.

He had finished his glass of port, and was considering the advisability of stimulating his brain further through this medium, when the hall boy entered to say that he was wanted on the telephone. The voice that spoke in his ear as he adjusted the receiver was that of Miss Pym.

"Sidney!"

"Hullo?"

"Are you there?"

"I am."

"Sidney!"

"Hullo?"

Miss Pym, who was plainly much stirred, now proceeded to utter about two hundred and fifty words in the space of time more customarily reserved for uttering ten, and Chibnall felt obliged to remonstrate.

"Who is this speaking?"

"Me, of course. Vera."

"Then don't talk like Donald Duck, my girl. You're fusing the wire."

Thus rebuked, Miss Pym applied the brakes.

"Sidney, it's those two men."

Chibnall started. This was more interesting. He had supposed when the conversation began, that he was merely about to listen to one of those rambling addresses to which his loved one, in common with so many of her sex, was so addicted when she took receiver in hand.

"Eh? What about them?"

"They're here."

"Where?"

"In my bar. Plotting."

"Then get back there and listen. Haven't you any sense?"

Miss Pym said that Chibnall needn't bite a girl's head off. Chibnall said that he had not bitten a girl's head off, but that every instant was precious. Miss Pym conceded this, but said that, be that as it might, there was no necessity to go biting a girl's head off.

"I'm going to listen," she said, wounded. "I've been listening."

"What did they say?"

"Nothing much. Well, they wouldn't, would they, with me there."

"You said they were plotting."

"I meant they were going to plot as soon as I was out of the way. So far, they've been talking about marriage."

"Marriage?"

"Yes. The thin one seemed to like it. The stout one didn't. Oh, Sid-*nee!*"

"Well?"

"The stout one's taken his moustache off!"

"What!"

"Yes. Not a trace of it left. Well, I'm going to listen now. I had to ring you up first and tell you. They're sitting right under that little sliding panel thing that you send the drinks into the lounge through by, and I'm going to open it an inch or two. I'll be able to hear all."

"Go on, then, and ring me the moment you have."

"All right, all right, all right, all right, all right," said Miss Pym, once more giving evidence that she was not her usual calm self. "What did you think I was going to do?"

She hung up the receiver and darted to the panel with rapid, silent footsteps, like Drexdale Drew in the Limehouse Mystery that time when he listened in on the conversation in the steel-panelled room at the Blue Chicken. Cautiously, she slid it open, and through the aperture there came a snatch of dialogue so significant that it was all she could do to stop herself giving a long, low whistle of astonishment. (Drexdale Drew, it will be remembered, was guilty of this imprudence on the occasion to which we have referred, and it was that that led to all the subsequent unpleasantness with the Faceless Fiend and the Thing In The Cellar.)

The dialogue ran as follows:

The Stout One: Then where is it?
The Thin One: Hidden in my room.
The Stout One: Well, go fetch it.
The Thin One: No, J.B. Before letting you get your hooks on it, I wish to talk turkey.

Miss Pym clung to the shelf below the little sliding panel thing that you send the drinks into the lounge through by, her ears standing straight up from the side of her head. This, she was telling herself, or the whole trend of the conversation had deceived her, was the real ginger.

The example of this girl in dismissing lightly, as if devoid of interest, the earlier portion of the interview between Joss Weatherby and Mr. Duff is one that cannot be followed by a conscientious historian. When two such minds are discussing a subject of such universal concern as the holy state of marriage, one must not scamp and abridge. It is not enough merely to say that the thin one seemed to like it and the stout one didn't. Their actual words must be placed on the record.

The conversation began in the lounge, where Joss, hastening

to the Rose and Crown, had found Mr. Duff huddled in a chair,
looking like an Epstein sculpture. The young man's opening
remark, as that of anybody else in his place would have done,
dealt with the new and improved conditions prevailing on his
elder's upper lip.

"Thank God!"

"Eh?"

"You've removed it?"

"She made me."

"Who?"

"Beatrice Chavender," said Mr. Duff glumly. He had not
particularly valued the moustache, but his proud spirit chafed
at coercion.

The mention of that name enabled Joss to bring up without
further delay the main subject on the agenda paper.

"Tell me, J.B., arising from that, is it true what they say
about Dixie?"

"Eh?"

"It's correct, is it, this story I hear about you being engaged?"

"That's what I wish someone would tell me."

"You are reported to have said you were."

"She acts as if I was."

"But you aren't sure?"

"No."

"I don't get you, J.B. You speak in riddles. Why aren't you
sure?"

"I don't seem able to figure out whether I really committed
myself or not."

"Come, come, J.B. You must know if you proposed to her."

"Oh, I didn't do that."

"Then what did you do?"

"Well, lemme tell you," said Mr. Duff.

He paused for a moment before proceeding. It was only too
plain that it cost him an effort to delve into the past. His attitude
towards the past seemed to resemble that of some timid diner
in a French restaurant, confronted with his first plate of bouilla-
baisse. He shrank from stirring it.

"Well, listen," he said at length. "It was like this. There I
was in bed, after the worst siege I've ever had. If I attempted to
describe to you the agonies I'd been suffering through the night,
you wouldn't believe me."

"But came the dawn, and you perked up?"

"No, I didn't. I felt like the devil. The pain had gone, but——"

"—It had left you weak. You were white and shaken. Like a sidecar. All right, push along."

"Don't bustle me."

"I want to get on to the sex interest. I'm waiting for the entrance of the female star. Did Mrs. Chavender come to you as you lay there?"

"Yes. And when the door suddenly opened and there she was, did it nearly slay me!"

"Whereupon——?"

"She said 'Gosh, Jimmy, you look like a rainy Sunday in Pittsburgh!' And I said 'I feel like a rainy Sunday in Pittsburgh.' And she said 'Have you been eating something that disagreed with you?' And I said 'And how!' And she said 'Poor old slob, your stomach always was weak, wasn't it? A king among men, but a pushover for the gastric juices, even in the old days.' "

"These were the first words you had exchanged in fifteen years?"

"Yes. Why?"

"I had often wondered what lovers said to one another when they met again after long parting. Now I know."

"I wish you wouldn't call us lovers."

"Well, aren't you?"

"I tell you that's what I'm trying to figure out."

"Did she smooth your pillow?"

"No."

"What did she do?"

"She went around to the drug store and brought me some stuff that tasted like weed killer. I'm not saying it didn't do me good. It did. But I'm still feeling as if someone had started a sewage plant in my mouth."

"And then——?"

"She sat down, and we kidded back and forth for a while."

"Along what lines?"

"Well, she said this, and I said that."

"That's a lot of help."

"What I mean, we talked of old times. Picking up the threads, as it were. 'Remember this?' 'Remember that?' 'Whatever became of old So-and-so?' You know the sort of thing. And then she asked me how I had got that way, and I told her."

"How did you get that way?"

"Well, it's a long story."

"Then don't tell it. Save it up for some evening when I'm head of the Art Department and you've asked me to drop in for dinner and a chat on general policy."

"Head of the Art Department?"

"That's what I said."

"Oh, yeah?" said Mr. Duff, with some spirit.

Joss forbore to press the point. It could wait.

"Well, so far," he said, "you seem to have come out of the thing with reasonable credit. If that was all that happened——"

"It wasn't."

"I thought the probe would dig up something sooner or later. What did happen?"

"Well, I'd finished telling her how I got that way, and she put her hand on my forehead——"

"I thought as much."

"——And said something about I ought to have a wife to look after me. And I said I guessed she was about right."

"Well, then! Well, there you are!"

"You think that committed me?" said Mr. Duff anxiously.

"Of course it committed you."

"I didn't mean anything personal," urged Mr. Duff. "I was just speaking in general terms."

"You need say no more, J.B. Order the wedding cake."

"Oh, gosh!"

"Buy the tickets for the honeymoon trip. Get measured for the hymeneal trousers. Sign up a good minister and make all the arrangements for conscripting the ushers. Good heavens," said Joss, "you go to infinite pains to spread the story that you wanted that portrait because you had been pining for this woman for fifteen years——"

"She hasn't heard that?"

"Of course she has heard it. The whole neighbourhood is ringing with it. Your fidelity is being held up as a mark for the male sex to shoot at by every female in the county. Do you really suppose that on top of a blast of propaganda like that you can tell Mrs. Chavender that you need a wife to look after you, and expect to carry on with your bachelor existence as if nothing had happened? You astound me, J.B. You're as good as brushing the rice out of your hair at the Niagara Falls Hotel already."

Mr. Duff rose. His face was drawn. He moved heavily.

"Come into the bar," he said. "I think I'd like a drink."

It seemed to Joss that Miss Pym, presiding at the fount of supply, was a little nervous in her manner as they stepped up to give their order. Her attractive eyes were large and round, and she showed a disposition to giggle in a rather febrile way. It occurred to him as a passing thought that something in the nature of a spiritual upheaval was taking place inside this puller of beer handles. But neither he nor his companion was in a mood to enquire too closely into the soul-states of barmaids. They withdrew with their tankards to a table at the side of the room— a table which, as Miss Pym was so swift to observe, was situated immediately below the little sliding panel thing.

It was Joss who resumed the conversation, opening it now on a cheerier and more encouraging note.

"What beats me, J.B., is why you are making all this heavy weather about a situation which should, one would have imagined, have set you twining flowers in your hair and doing buck-and-wing dances all over Loose Chippings. Can't you see how lucky you are? She's a wonderful woman. Looks. Brains. A delightful sense of humour. What more do you want? If you ask me, this is a far, far better thing that you do than you have ever done. This is where you begin to live."

Mr. Duff was not in the frame of mind to respond to pep talks. He continued sombre. His resemblance to something carved by Epstein on the morning after a New Year's party had increased rather than diminished.

"It's the whole idea of marriage that gives me that sinking feeling," he said. "It always did. When I proposed, I was thinking all the time what a sap I was making of myself. And when she bust our engagement, I went around singing like a lark."

It was not merely the nauseating thought of the other singing like a lark that caused Joss to shudder so violently that he spilled his beer. His whole soul was revolted by the man's mental outlook.

"Marriage is the most wonderful thing in the world," he cried warmly, "and only a sub-human cretin with a diseased mind could argue to the contrary. I appeal to you, Miss Pym," he said, arriving at the counter to have his tankard refilled.

"Pardon?" said Miss Pym, starting. She had been distraite.

"Isn't marriage a terrific institution?"

"Oo!" said Miss Pym, pouring beer in a flutter.

"Nothing like it, is there?"

"Coo!" said Miss Pym. "Excuse me," she added, and withdrew hastily. Joss returned to the table, feeling that he had made his point.

"You heard her reply to my question? 'Oo!' she said, and 'Coo!' Those words, straight from a barmaid's unspotted heart, are as complete an endorsement of my views as you could wish to have. You should take that soul of yours around the corner, J.B., and have it thoroughly cleaned and pressed."

"Look," said Mr. Duff, as impervious to honest scorn as he had been to encouragement. "When you get married, what happens? I'll tell you what happens. Government of the people, by the people, for the people, perishes from the earth. That's what happens. You get bossed. You can't call your soul your own. Look at the way she made me take off that moustache. It was a false one and I don't like moustaches anyway, but that shows you. And it's that sort of thing all the time, once you've let them poison-needle you and get you into the church. I like to smoke a mild cigar in bed before dropping off. That'll be out. Same with reading the evening paper at dinner. And what happens when I come back from the office, all tired out, and start reaching for my slippers? It'll be 'Snap into it and get dressed, Jimmy. Have you forgotten we're dining with the Wilburflosses?' Don't talk to me about marriage."

Joss shook his head.

"You paint a gloomy picture, J.B. I look at it in a different way. Let me sketch for you a typical day in my married life. I wake up, feeling like a giant refreshed. I spring under the cold shower. I climb merrily into my clothes, and down I go to a breakfast daintily served by loving hands and rendered additionally palatable by that smiling face peeping over the coffee-pot. Off to work, buoyed up by the thought that at last I've something worth working for. Perhaps we meet for a bite of lunch. Back to work again, right on my toes once more, with her gentle encouragement ringing in my ears. And then the long, restful evenings, listening to the radio and discussing the day's doings, or possibly——"

"Look," said Mr. Duff, who had been wrapped in thought. "I've had an idea. Seems to me there's a way out."

"I wish you wouldn't interrupt when I'm talking," said Joss, annoyed. "Now you've made me forget what I was going to say."

"Look."

"And another thing. Generally, when I meet you, you say 'Listen,' and now you're started saying 'Look.' I wish you would decide on some settled policy. One doesn't know where one is."

"Look," said Mr. Duff. "That time when we were engaged before, she called it off just because I happened to mention Paramount Ham once or twice. Well, look. What's she going to do when she finds out I'm using her portrait as a poster for the good old P.H.?"

Joss stared.

"You aren't going ahead with that scheme now?"

"I certainly am."

"I don't envy you when you tell her."

"I shan't tell her. I'll simply rush the thing through, and one fine morning she'll see the walls and bill-boards plastered with her face. And then what? I'll tell you what. She'll throw fifty-seven fits, and then she'll be on the phone to my office, asking what the hell. And I'll just raise my eyebrows——"

"Over the phone?"

"Over the phone. And I'll say 'Once and for all, I will not be dictated to. If I want to use your face to advertise Paramount Ham, I'll use it—see? If you don't like it, you know what you can do about it—see? Just like that."

"Over the phone?"

"Over the phone. Well, I'm here to tell you that if I know Beatrice, that'll be the finish. You brought the portrait with you?"

"No."

"But I told you to. Don't I get any co-operation? I distinctly said 'Go find that girl of yours—I keep forgetting her name—that little shrimp——' "

"I have had to speak to you before about this practice of yours of alluding to Miss Fairmile as a ——"

"—And get it from her, I said."

"I did get it from her."

"Then where is it?"

"Hidden in my room."

"Well, go fetch it."

"No, J.B. Before letting you get your hooks on it, I wish to talk turkey. You will now accompany me to Claines Hall, and

on the way I will state my terms. I warn you in advance that
they will be stiff."

At the address mentioned, Chibnall, too impatient to wait in
his pantry till the summons should come which he was expecting
every moment, stood tensely beside the telephone. The bell
shrilled in his ear.

"Hullo?"

"Sidney?"

"Speaking."

"Are you there?"

"Of course I'm here. Where did you think I was? Riding a
bicycle in Africa?"

"You needn't be a crosspatch."

"I am not a crosspatch."

"Yes, you are a crosspatch."

"I am sorry," said Chibnall, bringing to bear all the splendid
Chibnall self-restraint, "if I appear to be exasperated, but I am
anxious to hear from you your news with as little delay as
possible."

"Oo. Well——"

"Well?"

"Oo, Sid-nee, it's thrilling!"

"You heard something?"

"Did I! Coo! Talk about plotters!"

"Did they plot?"

"You bet they plotted. Sidney, that Weatherby has got something valuable hidden in his room. And the stout one wants it.
And they're coming to the Hall now."

"What!"

"I heard them say so. Weatherby is stating his terms on the
way. They haven't arranged yet how to divide the swag. What
are you going to do?"

Chibnall's jaw muscles were working menacingly.

"I'll tell you what I'm going to do. I'm going straight to that
Weatherby's room and search it from top to bottom. And when
they get there, they'll find me waiting for them."

"Oo! Sid-nee!"

"Yes?"

"They'll murder you."

"They won't. Because if they so much as start trying to, I'll jolly well murder them first. I'm going to get a gun from the gun-room."

"Oo!"

"I'll hide behind the curtains."

"Coo!"

"And pop out at 'em."

"Well, mind you're careful."

"I'll be careful."

"I don't want to be rung up from the Hall by Mrs. Ellis or someone and told that you've been found weltering in your blood."

Chibnall laughed lightly. He found these girlish tremors engaging. He liked women to be feminine.

"I shan't welter in my blood."

"Well, mind you don't," said Miss Pym.

19

T HE hour of nine-thirty found Claines Hall, dinner over, settled down to what Joss had described to Mr. Duff as the long, restful evening. Curtains had been drawn, lamps lit, the radio switched on to an organ recital, and Mrs. Steptoe and her Alsatian, Mrs. Chavender and her Pekinese, and Mr. Steptoe and a cat which liked his looks—which seems odd but cats are cats—and had attached itself to him in close comradeship, were seated about the library, occupied in their various ways.

Mrs. Steptoe was glancing through the morning paper, which until now she had had neither the leisure nor the inclination to peruse. The Alsatian was staring unpleasantly at the cat. The cat was sneering at the Alsatian. Mrs. Chavender was reading a novel and scratching her Pekinese's stomach. Mr. Steptoe, still practically a stretcher case after hearing what his wife had to say about men who shot craps with the flower of the County, was lying slumped in a chair, thinking of Hollywood.

Sally was not present. She had gone for a walk in the garden. And Lord Holbeton, unswerving in his resolve to be on the top step of the City and Home Counties Bank when that institution opened its doors for the transaction of business on the morrow, had already left for London.

Mrs. Steptoe, refreshed by cocktails and one of Mrs. Ellis's admirable dinners, was feeling better. The agony of that ruined garden party had abated, and the loathing for the human species which had animated her throughout the afternoon and evening had gradually dwindled, until now about the only member of it whom she would have disembowelled with genuine relish was Joss. She could not forgive his behaviour at their last meeting. In fact, she was not trying to.

She had just read in her paper a paragraph containing the hot news that Albert Philbrick (39) of Acacia Grove, Fulham, had been removed to hospital suffering from a broken rib and scalp wounds owing to falling down an excavation in the King's Road, Chelsea, and was just thinking in a dreamy way what a capital thing it would be if something like that could happen to the last of her husband's long line of valets, now presumably back in the metropolis, when the door opened and Chibnall appeared.

Supposing that he had merely flitted in, as butlers do flit in at about nine-thirty, to remove the coffee-cups, she was surprised when instead of buckling down to this domestic duty he advanced and took up his stand before her, coughing portentously.

"Could I speak to you, madam?"

"Yes, Chibnall? "

A closer student of the Greek Drama than Mrs. Steptoe would have been reminded of a Messenger bringing news from Troy, but even now she sensed nothing ominous in the atmosphere.

"It is with reference to the young man Weatherby, madam."

Mrs. Steptoe's tranquil mood was shot through by a quick twinge of irritation. She respected Chibnall. She had always thought him an excellent butler. But she found his conversation annoyingly limited in its range. It seemed to her that her recent life had been one long series of interviews with him which began with this preamble. She had a feeling that when she died, the words "It is with reference to the young man Weatherby, madam" would be found graven on her heart.

"Weatherby? Hasn't he gone?"

"Not yet, madam."

"Then get him out of here immediately," snapped Mrs. Steptoe, going briskly into her rattlesnake imitation. "I never heard of such a thing. When I fire someone——"

Mr. Steptoe came out of his coma with a start.

"Did you fire Weatherby, honey?"

"Yes, I did. And when I fire someone, I expect them to act like they were fired. So he's still here, is he, lounging about the place just as if——"

"No, madam. He is in the coal cellar."

"What!"

"I apprehended him and an associate burgling the house this evening, madam, and thought it advisable to lock them in the coal cellar."

It was a sensational announcement, and Chibnall knew it. It gratified him, accordingly, to note that it had gone over with solid effect. Apart from his own, and excluding those of the Pekinese, the Alsatian and the cat, there were three lower jaws in the room, and each had fallen to its furthest extent. In addition to this, Mr. Steptoe had uttered a low, choking cry.

"Burgling the house?"

"Yes, madam."

"Why was I not told about this before?"

"I thought it best to wait until after dinner, madam, in order not to interfere with your enjoyment of the meal."

This was obviously very decent and considerate of the man, and Mrs. Steptoe recognized it as such. She suspended that line of enquiry.

"Had they taken anything?" she asked, in a softer voice.

"Yes, madam. The portrait of Mrs. Chavender that hangs in the breakfast-room."

The Pekinese raised its head with a frown. The loving fingers which were kneading its stomach had administered an unpleasantly sharp jab.

"You don't say?" said Mrs. Steptoe.

"Yes, madam. I received information from a reliable source that the young man Weatherby was concealing something of value in his bedchamber, and I proceeded thither and instituted a rigorous search. I discovered the canvas hidden in a drawer and deposited it in my pantry. I then took up my station behind the curtain in the room, armed with a shot-gun, and waited. Eventually Weatherby arrived with his associate, and I apprehended them and conducted them to the coal cellar."

He paused modestly, like an orator waiting for the round of applause. It came in the shape of a marked tribute from Mrs. Steptoe.

"Nice work, Chibnall."

"Thank you, madam."

"Have you phoned the police?"

"Not yet, madam. I was awaiting your instructions."

"Go do it."

"Yes, madam. Should I bring Weatherby to you?"

"Why?"

"I gather that he wishes to make a statement."

"All right. Fetch him along."

"Very good, madam."

The stage wait which followed the butler's exit was filled in by a masterly *resumé* of the affair by Mrs. Steptoe, who like the detective in the final chapter of a thriller proceeded to sum up and strip the case of its last layers of mystery.

There had been a time, Mrs. Steptoe frankly confessed, when the machinations of the man Weatherby had perplexed her. She had guessed, of course, that he was up to some kind of phonus-bolonus, but if you had asked her what particular kind of phonus-bolonus she would not have been able to tell you. Everything was now crystal clear. This bimbo Weatherby was obviously a hireling in the pay of the bozo Duff, whom she had distrusted the moment she saw him. (You remember, Howard, when you found him sneaking around the place that time.) And it was her intention, after shipping Weatherby off to a dungeon, to bring an action against Duff for whatever it was—any good lawyer would tell her—and soak him for millions. This, in Mrs. Steptoe's view, would teach him.

All this took the form of a monologue, for neither Mr. Steptoe nor Mrs. Chavender seemed in the mood to contribute the remarks which would have turned it into a symposium. Mrs. Chavender was still scratching the Pekinese's stomach meditatively, while Mr. Steptoe paced the floor, his habit at times of mental unrest.

It seemed to Howard Steptoe that the curse had come upon him. Already he was solidly established in the doghouse as the result of that craps business. Into what inferno he would be plunged when this bird Weatherby arrived and started spilling the beans he shuddered to think.

His reverie was interrupted by the entrance of the bird Weatherby, escorted by Chibnall.

Joss was not looking his best. You cannot spend several hours in a coal cellar and be spruce. There was grime both on his hands and on his face. His cheerfulness, however, remained undiminished.

"Good evening," he said. "I must apologize for appearing before you like this, but my suggestion of a wash and brush up was vetoed by our good friend here. He seemed to think that speed was of the essence."

"You'll get a bath in prison," Mrs. Steptoe pointed out, possibly wishing to be consoling, though this was not suggested by her manner.

"Oh, we will hope it won't come to that."

"Will we?"

"Statement," said Chibnall in a curt aside. Throughout these exchanges, he had contrived with admirable skill to combine in his manner the inexorable rigidity of the G-man with the demure respectfulness of the butler. He was now for the moment pure G-man.

"Eh?"

"You told me you wished to make a statement."

"And I do wish to make a statement," said Joss heartily. "First, however, I would like to acquit my room-mate of the coal cellar of any complicity in this affair. He was merely a crony I had brought in for a smoke and a chat, and nobody more surprised than himself when he discovered that he was being held up with guns and placed among the anthracite. Dismiss him without a stain on his character, is my advice."

"Madam."

"Yes?"

"This is not true. My informant heard these two men plotting together. Their words left no room for doubt that they were in this game together up to the neck. Accomplices," said Chibnall, correcting with a slight blush this lapse from the purer English.

"Well never mind about the other fellow" said Mrs. Steptoe "What do you want to say?"

"This," said Joss. "I admit that I removed that portrait. But why did I?"

"I'll tell you."

"No, let me tell you. I painted that portrait myself. It was my own unaided work, and my masterpiece. Well, you know how artists feel when they paint masterpieces. They hate to let them go. If they let them go, they want them back. It was thus with me. The moment I parted with that portrait, I felt an irresistible urge to get it into my possession again. I had to have it. So I took it. Blame me, if you will——"

"I will."

"You will? I had hoped," said Joss reproachfully, "that a woman as sound on Corot as Mrs. Steptoe would understand and sympathize."

"Well, she doesn't."

"I shouldn't be surprised if Corot hadn't frequently done the same thing in his time. We artists are like that."

"And we Steptoes are like this. When we catch smooth young thugs looting the joint, we put them in the cooler. And that's what's going to happen to you, my friend. I don't believe a word of your story."

"But it's *good*." protested Joss.

"Go phone the police, Chibnall."

Howard Steptoe had stopped pacing the room. He was standing propped up against the table, trying to nerve himself to speak. The cat sprang on to the top of his head, unheeded.

The amazing discovery that this Weatherby, so far from spilling beans, intended to take the rap and go in silence to a prison cell had first stunned Howard Steptoe, then aroused all the latent nobility in his nature. Not normally a very emotional man, he found himself stirred to his depths. He saw that he must reveal all. To say that he liked the idea would be an overstatement, but he felt that he must do it.

And he was on the point of starting to do it, when Mrs. Chavender spoke.

"Just a minute, Mabel."

"Yes, Beatrice?"

"Mr. Weatherby did paint that portrait."

"Is that any reason why he should steal it?"

"That wasn't the reason why he stole it. He did it for me."

"No, no," cried Joss. "Don't listen to her. The woman's potty."

Mrs. Steptoe's china-blue eyes were wide with astonishment.

"For you?"

"Yes. I had to raise some money in a hurry, and I'm busted. I'm afraid I have misled you a little about my finances, Mabel. I lost practically all I had a couple of years ago."

"Delirium," said Joss. "Pay no attention."

Mrs. Steptoe blinked.

"You," she said, and paused.

"Are," she said, and paused again.

"Busted?" she said, her voice breaking in an incredulous squeak. "Is this a joke, Beatrice?"

"Not for me."

Mrs. Steptoe's face had been slowly turning bright red.

"Well!" she said.

"Still, after all," said Joss, "what's money?"

"Well!"

"You can't take it with you."

"Well!"

"It isn't money that counts, it's——"

"Well!" said Mrs. Steptoe. "I must say!"

She had sprung to her feet. The Alsatian, who came between

her and the carpet, uttered a yelp which drew a quiet smile from the cat.

"Well, I must say I wouldn't have expected you to be so deceitful, Beatrice. After this . . . Of course, this makes everything different . . . Of course, for poor Otis's sake, you can always have a home with me——"

"I knew you would be sweet about it, Mabel."

"But——"

"But," said Mrs. Chavender, "I expect my husband will want me to make my home with him."

"Your husband?"

"I'm going to marry Jimmy Duff."

"Oh!" said Mrs. Steptoe. She paused, plainly disconcerted. "He's very rich, isn't he?"

"Very."

"I should estimate J.B.'s annual income," said Joss, putting in his oar in his helpful way, "at around two hundred thousand dollars. It will be larger, of course, if he employs me."

Mrs. Steptoe eyed him coldly. The thought that she had been so injudicious as to treat as a poor relation a woman who was about to marry a millionaire was a bitter one, and she accepted thankfully this opportunity of working off some of her chagrin.

"If he's going to employ you," she said, "he'll have to wait a while. Your time's going to be occupied elsewhere for quite a spell. Chibnall, phone the police."

"Mabel, you can't do this."

"Can't I?"

"But, Mabel——"

Whatever appeal Mrs. Chavender had been intending to make to her sister-in-law's better nature was checked abruptly at its source. The air had suddenly become vocal with canine yelps and feline spittings.

Ever since he had been trodden on by Mrs. Steptoe, the Alsatian had been thinking things over and trying to fix the responsibility. It had now become plain to him that all the evidence pointed to the cat. He had never liked the cat. He had disapproved all along of admitting her to the library. But he had been prepared to tolerate her presence, provided she started no phonus-bolonus. This, by hypnotizing women into treading on his sore foot and smiling superciliously after it had occurred, she had done, and it was time, he felt, to act.

The cat, at the moment when he reached this decision, was still on top of Mr. Steptoe's head. It was consequently with something of a shock that the latter, whose attention had been riveted on his wife and Mrs. Chavender, became aware that a dog whom he had never liked was leaping up and scrabbling at his face. Nothing could actually affect his face, for better or for worse, but it was the principle of the thing that was important. He resented being used by this animal as a stepping-stone by which it could rise to higher things.

Nature had bestowed upon Howard Steptoe one gift of which he was modestly proud—his right upper cut. In the days when he had battled among the pork-and-beaners, he had too often been restricted in its use by the evasiveness of his opponents; but now, at last confronted by an antagonist who seemed willing to mix it, he was able to express himself. There was a dull, chunky sound, and the Alsatian, flying through the air, descended on an occasional table covered with china. Picking himself up, he sat surrounded by the debris, like Marius among the ruins of Carthage, and began licking himself. As far as the Alsatian was concerned, the war was over.

"How-WERD!" said Mrs. Steptoe.

There had been a time, and that recently, when the sound of his name, spoken by this woman in that tone of voice, would have been amply sufficient to reduce Mr. Steptoe to a shambling protoplasm. But now his eye was steady, his chin firm. He looked like a statue of Right Triumphing Over Wrong.

A man cannot have all the nobility aroused in him by the splendid behaviour of chivalrous valets, and on top of that win a notable one-punch victory over one of the animal kingdom, and still retain the old, crushed outlook. It was a revised and improved edition of Howard Steptoe that now stood tickling the cat behind the ear with one hand and making wide, defiant gestures with the other. Just after he has kay-oed an Alsatian, that is the moment when a hen-pecked husband is to be feared.

"Listen," he said, "what's all this about fetching cops?"

"I intend to send this man to prison."

"Do you?" said Mr. Steptoe, red about the eyes and bulging in the torso. "Is that a fact? Well, listen while I tell you something. This guy Weatherby is a right guy, and he doesn't go to any hoosegow, not while I have my strength."

"Well spoken, Steptoe," said Joss.

"The boy's good," said Mrs. Chavender.

"A fine fellow," said Joss. "I liked him from the first."

This excellent Press emboldened Mr. Steptoe to continue.

"Who does this portrait belong to? Me. Who's the interested party, then? Me. So who's got to prosecute if guys are to be slapped in the cooler for swiping it? Me. M-e, me," said Mr. Steptoe, who was all right at words of one syllable. "And I'm not going to prosecute—see? You know what I'm going to do? I'm going to hunt up Duff and sell him the thing."

"You won't have to hunt far," said Joss. "You will find him in the cellar."

"What!" said Mr. Steptoe.

"*What!*" said Mrs. Chavender.

"And I'm sure he will be charmed to do a deal."

Mrs. Chavender had risen, Peke in hand, and seldom in a long career of looking like Mrs. Siddons in Macbeth had she looked more like Mrs. Siddons in Macbeth than now. It is not given to many people to see an English butler cower, but that is what Chibnall did as her fine eyes scorched their way through him.

"What's that? Have you been shutting my Jimmy in your filthy coal cellar?"

Until this moment, Chibnall's attitude had been that of a detached and interested spectator. Basking in the background, he had been storing up in his mind every detail of this priceless scene in high life in order to be able to give Miss Pym a full eyewitness's description later. He had pictured her hanging on his lips as he reeled out sentences beginning with "He said" and "She said." That he might be swept into the swirl of the battle had not occurred to him, and now that this disaster had befallen, he was unable to meet it with the old poise. He gave at the knees, and looked sheepish.

"Er—yes, madam," he said, in a soft, meek voice.

There was an instant when it seemed as if Mrs. Chavender would strike him with the Pekinese. But she mastered her emotion.

"Take me to him immediately."

"Very good, madam. If you will come this way, madam."

The door closed. Mr. Steptoe resumed.

"Listen."

"Lemme tell you something," prompted Joss.

"Lemme tell you something," said Mr. Steptoe. "The moment

I've got Duff's dough in my jeans, this joint has seen the last of me. I'm going back to Hollywood, that's what I'm going to do, and if you've a morsel of sense you'll come with me. What you want, wasting your time in this darned place beats me. Nobody but stiffs for miles around. And look what happens to-day. You give this lawn party, and what do you get? Cloudbursts and thunderstorms. Where's the sense in sticking around in a climate like this? If you like being rained on, come to Hollywood and stand under the shower-bath."

"That's telling her," said Joss, awed. "That's talking."

Mrs. Steptoe, who had resumed her seat, was leaning forward with her chin in her hands, thinking. Like Joss, she had been profoundly stirred by this silver-tongued orator. Not if he had sat up at night for weeks, pruning and polishing and searching for the convincing argument, could Howard Steptoe have struck the right note more surely. He had put in a nutshell her very inmost thoughts.

"Listen," proceeded Mr. Steptoe, his voice now gentle and winning. "Just throw your mind back to Hollywood, honey. Think of that old sun. Think of that old surf at Malibu."

"That old Catalina," suggested Joss.

"That old Catalina," said Mr. Steptoe. "Say, you been to Hollywood?"

"Yes, I was there three years ago."

"Some place!"

"Considerable."

"You were a sap to come away."

"I'm glad I did."

"You're crazy."

"No. You see, Steptoe," said Joss, "love has found me. Which it wouldn't have done in that old Hollywood. Apropos of which, do you happen by any chance to know where Miss Fairmile is?"

"Said she was going out in the garden."

"Then I will be leaving you," said Joss. "Keep working," he added, in an encouraging whisper. "I think she's weakening."

For some moments after the door had closed, Mrs. Steptoe maintained her pensive reserve. Mr. Steptoe watched her anxiously. Presently she looked up.

"You know something, Howard?"

"Yes, honey?"

"I believe you're about right."

"You'll come?"

"I guess so."

"'At-a-girl!" said Mr. Steptoe. "'At-a-baby! 'At's the way to talk. 'At's the stuff I like to hear."

He clasped her to his bosom and showered burning kisses on her upturned face. Not even Joss, who was good at this, could have done it better.

20

SALLY'S walk in the garden had taken her to the wall of the moat, and when Joss found her she was leaning on it dejectedly, feeling out of tune with the lovely English twilight. Weeping skies would have been more in keeping with her mood. The weather is always in the wrong. This afternoon Mrs. Steptoe had blamed it for being wet. This evening Sally was reproaching it with being so fine.

The sound of Joss's footsteps made her turn, and at the sight of him she felt a faint flicker of hope. Her acquaintance with him, short though it had been, had given her considerable confidence in his ability to solve difficult problems.

"Well?"

He halted beside her.

"So here you are at my favourite spot. This is like old times. Remember?"

"I remember."

"You look more like a wood nymph than ever. It just shows."

"What?"

"I was thinking how utterly mistaken a man can be on matters outside his own business. J. B. Duff, for instance. He thinks you're a shrimp. One of these days, if the funds will run to it, I shall buy a pint of shrimps and show them to him. It seems the only way of convincing him. He repeated the monstrous statement this evening."

Sally started.

"You haven't seen him again?"

It came to Joss with a shock that this girl knew nothing of the tidal waves and earthquakes which had been giving his former employer the run-around and rocking Claines Hall to its foundations, and would have to be informed of what had occurred from the beginning. He paused, appalled at the immensity of the task. It was like finding someone who had never heard of the Great War.

"Oh, gosh!" he said.

Sally's worst forebodings were confirmed.

"Bad news?"

"Yes."

"Well, go on."

It was not a pleasant tale to have to tell, but he told it courageously, omitting nothing. When he had finished, he heard her teeth come together with a little click. There was a silence before she spoke.

"Then that's that?"

"I'm afraid so."

"You think Mrs. Steptoe is going back to Hollywood?"

"It looks like it."

"That means I shall have to go, too."

"Yes. I never thought of that at the time. I abetted and encouraged Steptoe in his insane scheme. I ought to be kicked."

"Are you sure Mr. Duff won't give you back your job?"

"Quite sure. He was peevish all through our sojourn in the cellar. He seemed to blame me for what had occurred."

Sally was silent again.

"Can't we get married and chance it?"

"On a capital of fifteen pounds and no job?"

"You'll get a job."

"Of course I shall," cried Joss. It was unlike him to remain despondent even for so long as this. His resilient nature reacted to her words like a horse that feels the spur. Nobody who had had the privilege of his acquaintance had ever mistaken him for anything but an optimist.

"There are lots of jobs."

"Millions of them, all over the place, just waiting to be got. I see now," said Joss, "where we have made our mistake. We have been looking on this Weatherby purely as an artist, forgetting how versatile he is. With you behind me, I don't see that there's anything I can't do. So everything's all right. I'm glad that's settled."

"What were you thinking of doing?"

"I can't tell you that till I have glanced through the Classified Telephone Directory."

"The only thing I can remember in the Classified Telephone Directory is Zinc Spelters."

"That may be what I shall decide on. Pots of money in it, I

expect. Can't you see us in our little home—you shaking up the cocktails, me lying back in the arm-chair with my tongue out? 'You look tired to-night, darling.' 'I am a little. This new consignment of zinc seems to take quite a bit of spelting. Not like the last lot.' "

"Oh, Joss!"

"Hullo?"

"I suppose you know I'm just going to commit suicide in the moat. I'm utterly miserable."

"Me, too, if you probe beneath the debonair exterior. I'm feeling like hell. I hope I haven't seemed too bright. When the bottom's dropped out of the world, I never know whether to try to keep up a shallow pretence that everything's grand or to let myself go and break down. But, honestly, why shouldn't I get something? I'm young and strong and willing for anything. Also—a point I was nearly forgetting—two can live as cheap as one."

"And money doesn't bring happiness."

"True. But, on the other hand, happiness doesn't bring money. You've got to think of that, too."

"I suppose so."

"Still, good Lord, when you look at some of the people who have got the stuff in sackfuls, you feel it must be pie to become rich. Take J. B. Duff. There's a case. Wears bank-notes next to the skin winter and summer, and yet, apart from a certain rude skill in the selling of ham, probably instinctive, as complete a fathead as ever drank bicarbonate of soda."

"Hey!"

The voice that spoke proceeded from a shadowy figure which had approached them unperceived. The visibility was now far from good, but the monosyllabic exclamation with which it had announced its presence rendered identification simple.

"Ah, J.B.," said Joss genially. "Torn yourself away from the little woman?"

Mr. Duff came to a halt, wheezing. His manner was not cordial.

"What was that you were saying about me?"

"I was telling Miss Fairmile here how rich you were."

"You said I was a fathead."

"And whom have you to blame for that, J.B.?" said Joss sternly. "Only yourself. Would anyone but a fathead have let a man like me go? If you would give me back my old job——"

Mr. Duff sighed heavily.

"It's worse than that. She says——'

"Who says?"

"Beatrice Chavender. We've just been chewing the fat, and she says I've got to make you head of the Art Department."

"Eek!" cried Sally, squeaking like a mouse surprised while eating cheese.

"Don't do that!" said Mr. Duff, quivering. "I'm nervous."

Joss, who had staggered so that he had been obliged to restore his balance by placing a hand on the wall, now laid this hand on the other's shoulder. His manner was urgent.

"You wouldn't fool me, J.B.? This is true?"

"That's what She says," said Mr. Duff lugubriously. "I told you how it would be. Bossed. Right from the start."

"Head of the Art Department?"

"So She says."

Joss drew a deep breath.

"Did you hear that, Sally?"

"I heard, Joss."

"Head of the Art Department. A position that carries with it a salary beyond the dreams of avarice."

"No, it doesn't," said Mr. Duff hastily.

"Well, we can discuss that later. Meanwhile," said Joss heartily, "let me be the first to congratulate you, J.B., on this rare bit of good fortune that has befallen you. You are getting a splendid man, one who will give selfless service to the dear old firm, who will think on his feet when its interests are at stake and strain every fibre of his being to promote those interests. I shouldn't be surprised if this did not prove to be a turning point in the fortunes of Duff and Trotter."

"She says I've got to have you paint my portrait."

"Better and better."

"And give that butler a wad of money to make him keep his mouth shut."

"Of course. We mustn't have him spreading the story of your shame all over the place. 'Tycoon In Coal Cellar' . . . 'Duff Dumped in Dust' . . . That wouldn't do. Stop his mouth, J.B. It will be money well spent. Gosh!" said Joss, "you've been doing yourself proud to-night, have you not? Thanks to you, my wedding bells will ring out. Thanks to you, Chibnall will now be able to buy that pub of his and team up with the Pym. Talk about spreading sweetness and light!"

"Ur," said Mr. Duff, not with much enthusiasm.

"It's sensational. Do you know what you remind me of, J.B.? One of those fat cherubs in those seventeenth-century pictures in the Louvre who hover above the happy lovers and pour down abundance on them. Take your clothes off, fit you out with a pair of wings and cornupia, and nobody could tell the difference."

Another long sigh escaped Mr. Duff.

"Fresher and fresher *and* fresher," he said sadly. "Well, I got to be getting back to Her. She's waiting to walk to the inn with me."

He turned, and was lost in the gathering dusk.

"Sally!" said Joss.

"Joss!" said Sally.

"My darling!" said Joss. "My angel! My own precious little blue-eyed rabbit!"

"Eh?" said Mr. Duff, reappearing.

"I wasn't talking to you," said Joss.

"Oh?" said Mr. Duff, and withdrew once more.

A rich contralto voice hailed him as he approached the front door.

"Is that you, Jimmy?"

"It's me."

"Did you see Weatherby?"

"I saw him."

"Then let's go," said Mrs. Chavender, chirrupping to her Pekinese. "It's a lovely evening for a walk."

This was indisputably true, but to Mr. Duff, as to Sally earlier, the fact brought no balm. As they made their way along the path that skirted the lawn, there rose from the wet earth like incense the fragrance of the sweet flowers of the night. All wasted on J.B. Duff. His heart continued heavy.

Mrs. Chavender, on the other hand, whose heart was light, sniffed appreciatively.

"Ah!"

"Eh?"

"Um!"

"Oh?" said Mr. Duff, getting her meaning.

"Stocks," said Mrs. Chavender. "You can't beat the scent of stocks."

"Swell smell," agreed Mr. Duff.

Mrs. Chavender seemed pleased by this poetic eulogy.

"You know, you've become a lot more spiritual since I first knew you, Jimmy. There's a sort of lyrical note in your conversation which used not to be there. About now, in the old days, if I had mentioned the scent of stocks, you would have been comparing it to its disadvantage with the smell of Paramount Ham in the early boiling stage."

"Ah," said Mr. Duff, sighing for the old days.

They walked on in silence for a moment.

"I want to talk to you about that, Jimmy."

"Ah?"

"Yes," said Mrs. Chavender, putting her arm through his. "I've been thinking quite a bit lately. Looking back, I can see that I must have been an awful disappointment to you in those days. I was a fool of a girl, and didn't know enough to be interested in higher things. Like ham. Do you remember me saying 'You and your darned old hams!' and throwing the ring at you?"

"Ah!" said Mr. Duff wistfully. He was oppressed by a dull feeling that breaks like that do not happen twice in a man's life.

"I've got sense now. You'll find me a wife that takes an interest in her husband's business. Yessir!"

For an instant, Mr. Duff's gloom lifted a little. Then the fog came down again. It was that operative word "husband" that was like a knell.

"Jimmy," said Mrs. Chavender, an earnest note coming into her voice, "let's talk about that portrait. Did you take a real good look at it?"

"Ah."

"Anything strike you about it?"

"How do you mean?"

"Listen, Jimmy," said Mrs. Chavender, "I was giving it the once over before I came out, and an idea hit me like a bullet. I believe I've got something. Here's what I thought. It seems to me people must be getting tired of seeing nothing but pretty girls in the advertisements of Paramount Ham. Isn't it about time you gave them something different? You may think I'm crazy, but I can see that portrait as a poster."

Mr. Duff had halted and was swaying gently, as if he had been pole-axed and could not make up his mind which way to fall. Her words seemed to come to him from far away.

"I don't know if you get what I mean. Here's what I was thinking. Maybe it was just a passing expression that Weatherby happened to catch, but in that portrait he's given me a sort of impatient, imperious look, as if I was mad about something and didn't intend to stand for it. And what I thought was that if you took the portrait just as it is and put underneath some gag like— well, for instance: 'Take this stuff away. I ordered Paramount!' you'd have a poster that got a new angle. Any good?" said Mrs. Chavender diffidently.

Nothing could ever make Mr. Duff's face really beautiful, but at these words it went some of the way. A sudden glow of ecstasy illuminated it like a lantern.

All that he had ever heard or read about soul-mates came back to him. All that he had ever thought and felt about the drawbacks of marriage surged into his mind, and it seemed incredible to him that he could have entertained such sentiments. Looking at it in its broad, general aspect, of course, he had been right. In the great majority of cases, a man who married proved himself thereby a sap of the first order, and he could understand how marriage had come to be referred to as the fate that is worse than death.

But where he had made his error was in not allowing for the special case. Grab the right partner, as he had so cleverly done, and you were sitting pretty. There lay before him in the years to come, he estimated, some nine thousand, two hundred and twenty-five breakfasts, and at each of these breakfasts he would see this woman's face across the table. And he liked it. He was heart and soul in favour of the thing. By careful attention to his health he hoped to make the total larger.

"Listen," he said huskily.

"Yes?"

"Will you do something for me?"

"Sure. What?"

"No, nothing," said Mr. Duff.

He had been about to ask her if she would gaze into his eyes and put a hand on each cheek and draw his face down to hers and whisper "My man!" but though feeling fine, he was not feeling quite fine enough for that. Later on, perhaps.

He drew her arm against his side with a loving pressure.

"Listen," he said. "Lemme tell you something about Paramount Ham. All through the slump years, when every other ham on the market was taking it on the chin and yelling for help, good old Paramount——"

The night covered them up.